Trail of the Hunter

TRAIL OF THE HUNTER

LEE MARTIN

AVALON BOOKS
THOMAS BOUREGY AND COMPANY, INC.
401 LAFAYETTE STREET
NEW YORK, NEW YORK 10003

© Copyright 1990 by Lee Martin
Library of Congress Catalog Card Number: 90-90338
ISBN 0-8034-8834-3

PRINTED IN THE UNITED STATES OF AMERICA
BY HADDON CRAFTSMEN, SCRANTON, PENNSYLVANIA

To my brother Don, a hard-riding, fast-roping man's man, who would have been at home in the Old West, and to his lovely wife, Barbara.

-

Chapter One

Clay Darringer bent low on his Texas saddle. He couldn't believe what he was seeing, not here in this barren land and desolate heat. His wide-brimmed Stetson shaded his steel-gray eyes as he peered down into Bravo Canyon.

Hundreds of feet below, down along the dry creek bed, a young woman in a green dress was staggering westward between the hot granite walls, barely keeping to the shade. Her long red-brown hair was spread over her face and shoulders.

Another mile and she would be at the waterhole at the mouth of the canyon, along with a dozen renegade Apaches.

Clay was determined to cut her off. His blue roan gelding, its hooves already blanket bound, picked its way carefully down a steep, narrow deer trail, rocks and dirt sliding around them. It was a dangerous descent.

He leaned far back in the saddle, sweat under his double-breasted blue shirt, his shoulder-length brown hair damp, a red bandanna loose about his strong neck.

A week's growth of dark beard covered the thin white scar on his left cheek. Square of jaw and with a slight hook to his nose, he was a tall and fierce but handsome man, with wide shoulders and a lean body.

Like his brothers, he was a gunfighter.

At his right hip was a .45 Army Colt. A Winchester repeater was in the scabbard and a hunting knife at his belt. At twenty-nine, he was a man's man in tough country. Arizona Territory in the fall of 1877 was no picnic ground.

Saddlebags, long leather coat, bedroll, and the canvas bag full of "possibles" bounced behind the cantle. Leather-bound metal canteens dangled from each side of the pommel.

Suddenly, the roan slid straight down ten feet, then recovered his footing for a moment. The horse shuddered.

"Easy, Blue," Clay urged.

The big horse skidded the rest of the way down into the canyon, barely keeping his balance. Lizards scattered from his path. Rocks rolled around the roan's powerful legs, his rump sliding in the dirt. Then the animal sprang onto the canyon floor, sweat on his thick neck.

There would be no retracing their path up that cliff.

Clay leaned from the saddle to be sure the blanket shoes were intact, laced up above the fetlocks. The tough Army wool had not suffered from the slide. He had tied them on to deaden sound, but now they would also smooth his trail.

He guided his mount across the shallow, dry creek

bed, up onto the far bank. Here the sun didn't reach him or the woman. She was coming toward him, swaying, with her head down. In her right hand was an old handgun.

He rode to her, reaching down with his left arm and scooping her up to rest in front of him. She struggled briefly as he held her against the pommel, then let her slump against him, her skirts spooking his mount. Her left hand painfully lifted to push against his chest.

"Quiet, ma'am," he murmured. "We got company."

She looked at him through fuzzy red-brown locks. Her eyes were grass-green, but he still couldn't see her face, except for the red bruise on her forehead. She rocked against his right arm, trying to speak through parched lips. She was breathing too fast.

He took the handgun, an old single-shot, and stuck it in his belt.

He gave her water from one of the canteens. She frantically grasped the metal can. Soon he had to drag it from her grasp. She slumped back against him, and he hooked the strap of the canteen over the saddle horn.

"We got to cool you off," he said.

He rode eastward, reining his mount back and forth, covering her tracks. They continued between the red rock walls, Clay watching the rims above.

It was likely that the twelve young Apaches were on their own, drunk with freedom. It was unlikely that they would head west to the open prairie. Instead, they would probably come through the canyon and head north into the sheltered rock country to reach the green mountains.

He saw a wisp of smoke in the passage, just ahead of them. Continuing slowly and cautiously through the narrow walls, he soon was in sight of a heavy spring wagon.

A campfire was smouldering on buffalo chips that must have been carried from the eastern plains. Three dead men lay under the wagon. There were no horses or mules in sight. The air was stagnant with an eerie silence.

Clay leaned from the saddle to read sign. Tracks surrounding the wagon were from shod horses and high-heeled boots. The prints made it obvious that five killers had followed the wagon, done their brutal deed, and then ridden back eastward. The team of horses had broken loose and headed in the other direction, toward the waterhole.

The wagon was choked with white dust and sand. It was apparent they had hit a sandstorm.

The footprints of the woman he was protecting came from under the wagon. He rode across them several times. He leaned over into the wagon bed and took two blankets, forcing them into the woman's arms.

"We can't bury 'em," he said quietly. "If we did, the Apaches would know someone from the wagon survived. We have to make sure they follow the killers, not us."

He rode slowly alongside but clear of the shod prints, knowing the canyon ran eastward another five miles. They had to get out of this trap.

It was then he saw the little dry creek on the left wall, running up through the rocks. There would barely be room for his horse, but it was a way to the rim nearly two hundred feet above.

The big roan was already bone weary, but its muscles responded as Clay turned it up the narrow path. The horse fought his way up the rocks and gravel, sliding and pawing upward. With great lunges, he cleared barriers.

The woman leaned forward, clinging to the short, fat horn. Clay bent close to her.

At the top at last, his mount sweating and panting, Clay slid from the saddle. He reached up and lifted her enough to set her astride. He forced the reins into her hot hands. The sun was brutal.

"It's all right now," he told her.

After checking the blanket shoes, he coaxed the roan forward. He followed, dragging one of the blankets over his own prints, staying several hundred feet from the rim to their left.

There was little vegetation on the bluff. Scrub brush and stunted junipers were scattered over the rocks and crimson earth.

They were soon near the edge of the ridge at the canyon entrance. The sun was bearing down unmercifully. At a small grove of junipers, he stopped the blue roan in the shade. The woman was gazing down at him without recognition.

"Wait here," he told her. "A dozen Apache down in the canyon."

She mouthed the word "Apaches?" without a sound.

"Last spring, they arrested Geronimo," he said, "and Victorio surrendered. But a few weeks ago, some White Mountain Apaches broke out. Seems nothin's been right since Clum left San Carlos."

Winchester in hand, he headed south on foot in the hot afternoon sun, reaching the rim of the canyon. Here he knelt, moving closer to the edge, then lying on his stomach.

Below, he could see the mouth of the canyon, where the waterhole was visible against the south wall in the shade. Beyond, the prairie spread green and red toward the western horizon. To the northwest, crimson-streaked yellow bluffs were set against a haze of foothills.

The twelve Apache were mounted. Some of the horses were Army. Being led were two heavy built horses with harness marks, obviously the missing team from the wagon.

The young men were not tall but had strong bodies and great chests. Their faces were square, with high cheekbones and keen eyes. Nearly naked, black hair to their shoulders, bronze skin glistening in the sun, they were handsome men. They were also in a good mood.

He watched them jostle each other. They were laughing. It was obvious that they were not particularly hunting white men this day. It was freedom that intoxicated them. They had old rifles and their bows and arrows, having returned to their traditional way of life.

The Apaches headed eastward up the canyon, setting their mounts into a lope, playfully zigzagging each other. Clay hoped they were covering any signs he might have left.

He hurried back over the rough terrain, reaching the weary roan and the dazed woman. It didn't take long to reach and descend the sloping trail at the end of the ridge.

The sun was still beastly hot. On the canyon floor, the red earth was cooler, the waterhole sheltered in the shade. He led the roan forward and let it drink a little at a time.

Reaching up, he put his big hands at the woman's small waist. He set her down in the shade near the water. He loosened the cinch on his weary mount, then returned to kneel at the woman's side.

With his big right hand, he spread aside the thick reddish-brown hair, moving it from her hot face. She was staring at him. Her features were delicate, even beautiful. There was a sprinkle of freckles on her cheeks. Her nose was slightly turned up at the end. She was at least twenty. Soft and fair.

He felt her cheek. Her skin was flushed, hot and dry. The red bruise on her forehead was turning blue. She was still breathing rapidly.

"Here, ma'am," he said, forcing the canteen to her lips.

Tasting the water, she lifted her trembling hands to grasp the metal can, holding it in place. He had to jerk it from her as she continued to swallow. He refilled it from the pond and hung it back on the saddle.

Then he knelt as the woman struggled to rise.

He removed his red bandanna, soaked it with

water, and then washed her hot face. She was confused, watching as he unbuttoned the waist-jacket part of her dress, exposing the white lace bodice beneath.

"I've got to cool you off," he told her.

Removing the jacket from her, he again used the wet bandanna on her face, throat, and shoulders. She was still breathing too quickly. He felt her throat. Her pulse was racing.

He turned her around and drew her to the water's edge, holding back her skirts as he pulled off her soft shoes and long stockings, shoving her hot legs and feet into the cool water. She gasped and slumped forward. Using the bandanna, he sloshed the wet on her back and neck.

Gradually, she took it from him, holding it to her face. Then she moved to kneel, dipping her face and hair in the water, trying to wash away the dirt.

He sat on his heels, looking eastward up the canyon.

There was no telling whether the Apaches might ignore the obvious shod tracks and instead follow Clay's trail over the rim. She gazed at him, wet hair clinging to her face. She was still disoriented. He rubbed bear grease on her cheeks and nose.

"Don't worry," he said, his voice low.

It was mighty hot. Sundown was hours away. He knew they had to go. He cinched up his mount and hung his possible sack from the horn on the right side.

Returning to the woman, he helped her dress. Then he lifted her in his arms. Her head rolled against his chest as he carried her back to his horse. She was cooler now, breathing normally. He was more worried about her mind, having seen women survivors remain in a silent world.

The animal shied as Clay set her astride the fat bed-roll and saddlebags, behind the cantle, which she gripped frantically. Her skirts billowed behind and around her. The roan kicked a little.

Clay mounted, then pulled her arms around him. She clasped her fingers together at his belt. Her head rested against his damp back. He rolled the extra blankets in front of him.

He guided his tired mount toward the open prairies, but headed northwest toward the distant red and yellow bluffs.

"We got to get some cover," he said, his voice low.

But for his mumblings and the soft tread of his mount in the red earth, the prairie was deathly silent. Not an antelope or rattler stirred in the desolation. A lone buzzard was circling the distant western prairie.

The woman clung to him without response, but each time he spoke, she tightened her grip, her face pressed to his back.

Now they were approaching the main wagon road that ran east toward Santa Fe and west toward Prescott. Deep ruts were cut in the soil. Heavy freight wagons had been this way. There was no sign of life in any direction.

Clay rode into the path of the ruts, working his way to the other side, then continued northwest toward the bluffs.

"You got a name, ma'am?" he asked.

There was no answer, and he began to talk about himself, figuring it was all right, since she probably didn't understand his words. It was the sound of his voice that she needed.

"Me," he said, "I'm Clay Darringer, from Texas. Reckon I have three brothers. Ben, the oldest, he's a lawyer, got me and Hank that pardon a few weeks back."

Again, she tightened her hold on him, and he continued, encouraged that his deep, steady voice might be giving her comfort.

"My younger brother Jess, he's the musical one. Me, I guess I thought I was going to be a doctor."

Her face pressed harder at his back. He cleared his throat, his eye on the canteen dangling from the horn.

" 'Course we have a Ma down in Texas," he added. "And some half brothers and sisters."

Talking about his family made him homesick. He thought of Texas. His mother's face appeared in his mind, and he fell silent. He was glad when twilight brought them closer to the bluffs. It was cooler now.

In between the crimson walls, he found a hollow in one of them, worn by the wind. It was like a half cave, at least ten feet into the bluff. He slid from the saddle and reached up to lower the woman, his hands at her waist.

She gazed at him unseeingly. He caught her up in his arms and set her against the back wall on the blanket he had been dragging, wrapping the other spare around her. Night was falling fast. It would be mighty cold. He'd have to risk a fire, which he built of gathered brush in a hole he dug, surrounded by rocks.

The little smoldering fire was pungent but gave warmth. She was still in a daze, but had escaped heat-stroke. When he fixed beans and coffee, she did eat, but in silence.

Still trying to set her at ease and bring her back to reality, he continued his story.

"When I was on the dodge, I scouted for the Army. The Apache had a tough time shaking me. Got so they would deliberately leave messages to taunt me. I reckon if I'd have gotten killed, they'd have been mighty disappointed."

He suddenly felt that he was bragging. Yet it felt good to talk. Maybe it was because he had been alone for weeks on the prairie, crossing from Texas to Arizona Territory.

"You ever been to Kentucky?" he asked, changing the subject. "I read they got a big horse race there at Louisville. They call it the Kentucky Derby."

He refilled their coffee cups. She continued to stare at him as he talked.

"And you know, I was reading how they've even graduated a black man from West Point. Someday, folks won't even remember there was a War between the States. But then there's other troubles startin'. In California, they've got riots over cheap Chinese labor. In Pittsburgh, they called out the Army when the railroad strikes got out of hand."

She curled into her blankets, still silent and distant, but watching him, listening to his deep voice.

"But the newspapers got other things in 'em. Why,

back East, they're playing some game called baseball, hitting some little ball with a big stick, then everyone runnin' to get it. Don't make much sense, does it?"

She closed her eyes, and fell asleep at once.

After building up the fire, he pulled on his leather coat and wrapped a blanket around himself. He sat at the edge of the bluff where he could see the moonlit prairie.

The night was bitterly cold. Before dawn, he returned to the fire and heated up the coffee and beans. He then knelt at her side, shaking her gently by the shoulder.

Frantic, she sat up, drawing back to the wall, staring at him wildly. She looked around quickly, as if searching for the gun, and grabbed a rock.

"I'm a friend," he said, sitting back on his heels.

Closing her eyes a moment, shaking her head, she then stared at him with slow, hesitant recognition.

"Who are you?" she asked.

"Clay Darringer."

"Oh, the gunfighter."

She lowered the rock and accepted a cup of hot coffee, sipping from it. Her face was mighty pretty. He liked her freckles. The red in her hair was bright in the flickering flames. Her voice was soft and pleasing. Most fascinating, however, were her shining green eyes.

"You have a name, ma'am?"

"Katherine Turner."

"That your family at the wagon?"

"My brother Sid and two hired hands," she said, tears trickling down her cheeks. "Some men with bandannas over their faces came before daylight. One of them grabbed me and I fought, even pulling off his mask. I shot him, but he clubbed me down with his rifle. It was Sheb Wiley."

Clay gave her a plate of beans, but she continued her story, poking at the food with her spoon, her tears unheeded.

"When I came to, I was still pretty much out of my head. No one else was alive. The killers were gone. I took the gun and started to follow them."

"To do what?"

"I don't know."

"It wasn't loaded, and they went the other way."

She made a face, shaking her head as she thought this over. He reached over and filled her cup with more coffee. She sniffed back her tears and ate quietly, then spoke again.

"When Sid met me at Camp Grant," she continued, "we saw a herd of cattle moving north. My brother went over and talked to the men. He said one of them was Sheb Wiley. They went on north but Sid was worried, so we came this way instead. They must have followed us."

"You know this country?"

"Not exactly. I'm from Kansas, but two years ago, I went to Castle Creek to see my brothers. Jacob and Sid have been running the ranch since my father was killed by Apache over ten years ago. We have the best grass and a river. Everyone wants to buy us out, especially the Wileys."

"How is it you have the best land?"

"My father claimed it in 'sixty-five, eight years before the Apaches went to Camp Verde. The other ranchers came later when it was safe."

Clay leaned over to stoke the fire as she talked.

"If you'll take me to Castle Creek, Jacob will hire you to help us get Sheb Wiley."

"I reckon you'll need more than your testimony if you want a conviction. They may not believe you."

"Conviction? I thought you were a gunfighter."

"I'm not a killer."

"That's right. You said you wanted to be a doctor. Did you go to medical school?"

"Not exactly. I studied with a surgeon. But I gave up the idea. Look, ma'am—"

"Katherine."

"Look, Katherine, I'll take you to Castle Creek. It's only three days north. When we get there, you can talk to the local law. Then I'll be on my way to California."

"You saved my life. You have some responsibility."

Clay studied her. He sipped his coffee. She was outspoken, but she was mighty pretty, even with her hair such a mess and with the bruise on her forehead. He might eventually decide to help her, yes, but Clay never did anything like that in a hurry.

Like the tracker and hunter he was, he took every sign a step at a time.

"You said you had a pardon," she said, watching him.

He shrugged, wondering why he wanted to explain. "Well, some years back, Hank and I tried to help a widow run off some carpetbaggers. There was a fight. Hank and I got thrown in jail."

"Sounds like Texas gallantry," she said.

"Maybe, but we were about to be hung when Ben got us out. Just a month ago, he got the governor to pardon us. Ben's a good lawyer. Hank, he's wearin' a badge in Dakota. My other brother, Jess, he follows the trail herds."

"So there's four of you."

"And some half brothers and sisters."

"But you're different from the rest," she told him.

"How you figure that?"

She smiled, sipping her coffee, her eyes glistening.

"Are you married?" she asked.

"I lost my wife a year ago," he said.

"I'm sorry. How did it happen?"

"Childbirth. Lost 'em both."

"I'm so sorry," she said softly.

Uncomfortable, he set his cup aside and picked up the Winchester and stood. He walked back to the edge of the bluff, gazing across the prairie. The early light was sweeping the silver sage and red earth. There was no sign of the Apaches.

Returning to the camp, he discovered her desperately trying to comb her hair with a twig. She stopped at the sight of him. Embarrassed, she blushed with a slight smile. It was then he saw her dimples.

"We'd best move on," he said. "There's a farm station on the way where you can get some clothes."

"You mean, if the Apaches didn't stop there."

"It's Boxer's place. He lets the Apaches water their horses and take all the corn they want."

"Lets them?" she asked.

"Well, you got the idea. Apache don't need to ask, but it seems to suit them to treat the Boxers civil. Heard tell Mrs. Boxer cooks up some mighty good cornbread that's a real treat for them."

He saddled his roan but didn't bother with the blanket shoes, shoving them into his possible sack, which he hung over the horn. He broke camp, covering the fire as best he could, then set Katherine up on the bedroll once more, her legs humped over the saddlebags.

Clinging to the cantle, she sat precariously as he swung into the saddle. Timidly, she slid her arms around his waist.

"I never thanked you," she said. "I saw you come down the ridge. You could have gotten away."

Clay didn't answer as he turned his roan.

It was a long day in the saddle as they continued north. Rests were brief. Toward the end of the day, she began to press her face against his back. Once he felt dampness on his shirt. He knew she was crying.

Clay couldn't handle a woman's tears. It brought back painful memories. And once, an old man had told him a woman never cried just for herself, always feeling pain for those she loved even in her own misery.

The far hills were crowding the horizons on both sides. Wooded and cool, those hills offered water. Tomorrow, they would be at Boxer's. Rolling land was swallowing them now. Brown grass was tall and plentiful. Mesquite lined the washes. Sycamores and cypress appeared in the hollows.

Turning west into the hills, they made camp in a narrow canyon. Thick green junipers sheltered them. Water was trickling down the south wall from a spring. Clay collected enough in his Stetson to water his horse. They soon settled down by a crackling fire hidden deep in the rocks. The night was cold around them.

Somewhere in the darkness, a coyote was howling at the moon. In the surrounding terrain, night creatures rustled for food.

Katherine huddled near Clay and the warm fire, blankets pulled around her. Gripping the tin cup filled with steaming coffee, she sipped it carefully, lost in thought.

"You realize," he said, "that when you show up alive, your life may not be worth a hoot."

"I'm not afraid," she said with bravado.

"It didn't make sense for the Wileys to go after you, anyway. Why hunt you down out here?"

"Maybe they thought they could get away with it. They tried courting me, you know. Sheb and his brother Tuck, thinking they could get our land that way. Jacob ran them off."

"Just because they were Wileys?"

"There's a little more to it than that. You see, my family was for the Union. The Wileys are Texans."

"So am I."

"There's a difference," she insisted, but did not elaborate.

Clay shrugged, sorry that the war would not be over for a long time. Hard feelings were hidden in the breasts of every man who came West after the conflict.

She lay near the fire, rolling more deeply into her blankets. The light brought out the red lights in her thick hair. Wrapping himself in a blanket, over his leather coat, Clay sat against the passage wall, his Winchester in hand, sleeping off and on, trying to stay alert.

The roan was standing nearby, hobbled.

When dawn was less than two hours away and Clay was dozing, he heard the quick yip of a coyote. Only this time, it wasn't a coyote.

He tensed, rifle ready, heart pounding.

Chapter Two

*C*lay didn't know how close the Apache were. Maybe they only smelled the smoke and had yet to find the camp. It was still more than an hour before dawn.

Quickly, he sprang to his feet, moving over to the roan. He saddled the horse and loaded his gear.

Again, the false cry of a coyote. South. Both were south, quite a distance. Maybe Clay and the woman were not the target. Maybe snakes didn't bite.

Clay knelt and awakened Katherine, his hand over her mouth as he pulled her to her feet and half-dragged her to the horse. She stumbled along at his side. He lifted her into the saddle, setting her down astride with the blanket still around her, handing her the reins.

"Ride straight north," he whispered, pointing. "They show up, you take off as fast as you can and don't look back."

After kicking dirt over the fire to bury it, he used a blanket to wipe out signs of the camp. Still, he knew the Apaches could smell it. He dragged the blanket

19

behind him as he followed her. The Winchester was heavy in his hand.

There was sweat on his face, down into his beard.

If God was with them, they would get away without leaving a trace. Yet he knew how well the Apache could track. His best chance was to get Katherine to Boxer's ranch.

The moon was three-quarters full. Clouds cut its glow now and then, but they were making good time. It was bitter cold.

At first light, the sky was turning silver. Pines shadowed them on either side as they made their way north through the passage.

Daylight found them still in the long canyon full of trees and grass. At Clay's instructions, Katherine kept the horse in the soft dirt.

The sky was darkening. Rain and mud would make it harder to hide their tracks, but it might slow the trackers.

"Turn left, through that other canyon," Clay said in a low voice.

Dutifully, she reined the horse to the left. The canyon was similar, but with more cottonwoods. The walls were yellow and white with streaks of red. There was less and less of the soft dirt it was so easy to sweep with the blanket.

Now they were out in the open. Cornfields spread before them. Stalks had been picked clean. Up on a knoll, north of the fields and a running creek, was a big adobe house. Smoke was trailing from the chimney. In the corrals, two chunky workhorses were standing next to a pair of saddle horses and a milk cow.

Near the corrals were about three dozen Army enlisted men standing with their horses. They were fresh-faced and mostly young, their blue uniforms neat and clean.

At the railing in front of the house were two cavalry horses, a mule, and a handsome bay gelding. On the bay was a fancy Mexican saddle, set with silver conchos. The bridle was just as decorated.

It was drizzling, the sky dark and threatening.

Clay led the roan to the corral and water trough. He lifted Katherine down, then unsaddled. Leaving the weary horse in a separate corral and his gear on a bench, he led her to the house.

Boxer greeted them at the door. He was a fat, jolly man with no hair. His blue eyes were little and round, like his mouth. Inside the cluttered, huge room, they met his short, plump, and jolly wife, a blond woman in a baggy dress with a pan of steaming cornbread in her hands. An iron oven was set in the hearth.

"Just in time," she said.

Clay turned to look around the room. Standing near the front window was a young lieutenant, his face round and pink. His shiny saber hung alongside his yellow striped britches. Next to him was a grizzled, stumpy sergeant who brightened in recognition.

"Clay Smith! Lieutenant, this is the scout I was telling you about. The one the Apache called the Hunter!"

Clay grinned at the man with whom he had enjoyed wrestling, playing cards, and sharing tall tales.

Then he saw a dazed youth of about fourteen years, sitting in the corner with his arms folded.

"The boy is Wes Barnes," the lieutenant said, shaking Clay's hand. "We came across his family diggings east of here. He was the only survivor."

"Apaches?" Clay asked.

"Yes," the officer said, glancing at Katherine.

"This is Miss Turner," Clay said. "Her brother and his men were killed by outlaws a couple days south in Bravo Canyon. It'd be appreciated if you would bury them."

"I'll make it a point," the officer promised.

"I'm taking her to Castle Creek, unless you're headed there."

"No, we just came from San Carlos. We're going south," the officer replied. "Victorio broke out. I'd be obliged if you took the boy with you. That's his mule out there. Unless you're coming with us?"

"Can't," Clay said. "But I'll take the boy."

Clay shook the sergeant's hand as the officer went out the door.

"We had some times," the grizzled man said, grinning.

"I figure you still owe me on that last hand of poker," Clay reminded.

"You mean when Geronimo jumped us? We hightailed it so fast, I don't even know who was winnin'."

"Take my word for it," Clay said, grinning.

The sergeant just laughed and followed the lieutenant outside, closing the door behind him. Clay was still grinning at his memories of being around the soldiers. They were all good men with guts.

He turned to Mrs. Boxer, who was fussing over Katherine.

"I was wondering if you had anything Miss Turner might be able to wear," Clay said, as he sat down at the table.

"Well, sure," the woman replied. "I got things I can't fit no more. We even got a big tub she can wash in. Soon's that feller comes out. But don't you worry, honey. You'll have fresh water."

"Feller with the fancy saddle," Boxer said.

Clay leaned back as she served him and Boxer some hot coffee. He glanced toward the closed door in the far corner.

"Meanwhile," the woman said to Katherine, "we'll see what I can find for you."

Timidly, Katherine followed the woman into the back bedroom.

"A couple Apache were trailing us on the way here," Clay said. "Maybe we lost 'em."

"You believe that?" Boxer asked.

"No."

Abruptly, the far door that apparently led to a bathtub swung open. Out walked a slim man of average height, dressed in black, with silver conchos on his gunbelt and hatband.

Clay felt a warning flash through his mind.

The man was clean-shaven, except for a thin black mustache. His eyes were nearly black. His face was lean, with wrinkles on each side of his mouth and across his brow. His nose was thin. He was maybe thirty. He wore two sidearms. There was a sneer about him even as he smiled.

"Clay Smith," Boxer said, "this is Jace Carmody."

Instantly, Clay went cold down to his boots. Carmody, the fast gun from Wyoming. He would never know why, but he had to give his correct name.

"Clay Darringer," he said.

Carmody's smile was slimy, his mouth curving down, then up at the corners. His dark eyes narrowed. There was pleasure in his face. Carmody was a dangerous man, from his cold mannerisms to his fearless approach.

The two men looked each other over. Carmody pushed his hat back from his brow. Then he offered a slim hand with long fingers.

Clay declined to tie up his gun hand and merely nodded. Carmody's smile broadened but his lips remained thin and narrow.

Boxer, looking from one to the other, was just beginning to grasp the situation. He began to chatter, offering them cornbread and more coffee.

Carmody sat down opposite Clay, Boxer between them. The table was maybe four feet across, but the distance felt like four inches. He and Carmody never took their eyes off each other as they talked about the departing soldiers.

"Clay was known as the Hunter, 'counta he's such a good tracker and never gave up," Boxer said. "The Apaches never could get away from him."

"Not true," Clay insisted. "But I did all right."

The men sat quiet as Mrs. Boxer carried two kettles of hot water to the smaller back room, then returned for more. Boxer brought in more water from the outside well. Soon the fat woman disappeared.

Clay tried not to think of what was going on behind closed doors.

"Now, that's a right comely young woman you brought here, Clay," Boxer said.

"She's been pretty brave," Clay said, feeling his beard.

"Well, I don't want to scare the young lady," Boxer added, "or my wife, but the sooner you high-tail it north, the better."

"You got trouble here?" Clay asked.

"Just a smell. Them Apache been testy of late. Sure glad the Army didn't stick around. And your bein' here, well, they'd love to get their hands on you. I'd take it as a favor if you'd all head out."

"My horse can't carry double much longer," Clay said.

"Then take the little sorrel mare out there," Boxer offered. "She was my wife's horse, but nowadays she can't hold up under the saddle, if you know what I mean."

Clay reached in his shirt pocket and drew out a ten-dollar gold piece. "This do it?"

"No need for that. She was given to us. And gold ain't gonna do us any good if there's trouble."

"Take it," Clay insisted.

With a grunt, Boxer took a piece of paper and lead pencil, writing out a bill of sale and exchanging it for the gold. Clay slid the paper in his shirt pocket.

All the while, he and Carmody kept watching each other.

"All right, Clay," Boxer said. "Now you just put

on that old Mexican saddle that's in the shed and move out."

"Without more of that cornbread?"

Boxer grinned and cut three big pieces from the hot pan.

"Them Apaches sure like this," Boxer said, passing the butter. "They'll probably tie me over an anthill but sure enough, they'll just make her chief cook."

"Nothin' to joke about," Clay said.

"You're right," Boxer agreed, sobering for the first time.

For a moment, they paused to listen to the rain on the roof. Despite the fire in the hearth, the room felt cold.

They talked awhile about Texas and reconstruction. Carmody talked about Wyoming and the vigilantes.

The war entered the conversation, as did the Army. But Clay was concerned about Victorio having left San Carlos.

"Maybe," Clay said to Boxer, "you ought to pack up and head for Castle Creek."

"What, and show weakness? That's all them Apaches need. They'd be on us like flies on a hog."

"Have it your way."

"This place is all we got, Clay. Corn grows tall and healthy. We got plenty of water."

Carmody leaned back in his chair as he spoke to Clay. "I'm on my way to Castle Creek myself. If you got a lady with you, and that boy, maybe we ought to ride together."

"I'd appreciate it," Clay said.

Turning in his chair, Clay glanced at the boy. He noted the confused expression and clammy skin. Probable concussion, he thought, noting the dark bruise on the lad's forehead.

The door to the room with the bath suddenly opened, and Mrs. Boxer stood there with a big grin. After a moment, Katherine appeared.

Clay nearly dropped his coffee cup.

Wearing a blue silk dress with white lace at the throat and wrists and tight at the waist, Katherine was stunning. Her sparkling clean, dark red hair was brushed in gorgeous sweeps away from her lovely face.

Carmody immediately stood up, removing his hat.

She was too beautiful. Clay, still seated, peered into his cup and spoke gruffly.

"You gonna ride in that?"

"Now, Clay," Mrs. Boxer scolded, "you know she ain't. I just wanted you to see how she's gonna look when you get to town. I'm gonna give her a ridin' skirt I made. Even though it ain't fittin' to ride astride, I found a woman got no choice out here."

Still uneasy, Clay looked up again. Katherine was so lovely and feminine, he couldn't match her with the dazed and dirt-covered woman he had found. Even her hair had turned out to be all red.

And Clay didn't much appreciate the way Carmody was looking her over and bowing ever so slightly.

Katherine turned and went back into the bedroom with Mrs. Boxer, the door closing behind them. Clay suddenly realized he had been holding his breath.

"What you gonna do with her?" Boxer asked.

"Get her to Castle Creek, that's all."

Carmody sat down. "Is that all you can think of?"

"Well, Clay," Boxer said, "the least you could do is shave."

Clay hesitated. He refused to think he would consider shaving because of Katherine. Still, he was going to town and would be among civilized people. He didn't smell too good, and he was mighty hairy.

Clay nodded. "Maybe you got some hot water left in one of the kettles."

Clay took a wash pan and set about shaving off his thick growth of dark beard, keeping his eye on Carmody. Clay's skin was tender to the blade, but soon he was clean-shaven once more. The thin white scar on his left cheek was visible again.

Boxer made sure the small room with the tub was empty, and Clay was able to bathe. He felt almost human when he returned to join Boxer and Carmody. The women were still in the bedroom.

"Women love to talk," Boxer said. "Funny thing is, I kinda like to listen to 'em. Makes a man feel at home."

Clay glanced at Carmody. Although he didn't fully trust him, he knew the gunman would be an asset if they ran into Apaches. He was getting curious, though, as to why Carmody was heading for Castle Creek.

Boxer served more coffee. Then the women returned to the room. Katherine was wearing a blue riding skirt and jacket. With her shining hair and clean face, she still looked lovely.

Clay hadn't expected such a change in her. It threw him. She, in turn, was startled by his missing beard.

Carmody stood up to offer her a chair, holding it for her. She smiled her thanks and sat down. The gunman pulled up another chair between her and Clay, who was annoyed. Boxer introduced the gunman.

During a hefty meal with the Boxers, the conversation was light and friendly, centering mostly on Carmody's tales of Wyoming. The youth was quiet, listening to the stories.

"Now it really doesn't make sense," Carmody was saying, "that women should have the vote. Some feller named Bright caused the whole thing. His name just didn't fit what he did. I mean, you can just figure the wife's gonna vote like her husband says, so he has two votes."

Katherine came to life, green eyes sparkling.

"That's what the husband may think," she said. "But it's a secret ballot, remember?"

Carmody smiled. "You mean you'd vote against your husband?"

"If I had one, and disagreed, yes," she insisted.

The conversation became lively. Carmody loved baiting Katherine. The gunman was so taken with her that Clay abruptly decided it was time to leave. The youth was the first one out the door.

"I was sure glad to meet you," Mrs. Boxer said to Katherine. "I liked hearing about Kansas."

The women hugged, and Katherine followed Clay and Carmody outside. Still silent, Wes climbed onto his mule.

The rain had stopped. The Boxers had given them old slickers, which they tied behind the saddles as the sky was clearing. Carmody was already outfitted. He sat astride his bay, waiting.

The sorrel mare had white stockings and a bald face. It was light of foot, prancing and tossing its head. Clay was worried because he knew it had not been ridden for a long time, but to his surprise, Katherine was a good horsewoman. As she sat the saddle, the sorrel reared, pawing the air. She brought the horse back down gently without sawing its mouth.

Behind Katherine's cantle, a carpetbag was tied down, heavy with clothes and shoes.

They would be another night on the trail. Clay hoped the Apache had lost their scent, but he was less concerned now that Carmody was riding with them.

He rode through the green and red hills, keeping ahead of her, the little sorrel no match for his big roan's stride. Katherine was forced to trail. Carmody and Wes brought up the rear.

Big bushes of sage with tiny yellow flowers mingled with pinyon pines, tall junipers, and golden aspens. Rabbit brush in heaps of growth were dotted with smelly yellow blooms. A noisy blue jay scolded them as they passed its home in a tall pinyon pine. A horned toad lay on the rocks, watching the riders pass.

The sky was clear overhead, but dark clouds still lay on the western horizon. Clay kept a watchful gaze on the surrounding terrain.

The others followed him up through the rocks and

onto a level plain. Shadows were deep. It was getting cold. At length, Clay found a hollow between a rise of boulders.

They made camp, the men unsaddling. Still weary, Katherine gratefully sat down with blankets around her. Clay reluctantly built a small fire, deep in a circle of rocks he stacked, to keep her warm. The days were hot, but nights were bitterly cold.

Clay knelt by the youth, who just stared at him.

"How did it happen, Wes?" Clay asked.

"When the Apaches came, I was riding in from the mine. They shot my horse and it threw me into the rocks. When I came to, it was all over. Guess they thought I was dead."

"You may have a concussion," Clay told him. "Do you have any double vision?"

"Not now," the youth said. "My headache's gone too."

"Are you a doctor?" Carmody asked, amused.

"He studied medicine," Katherine said.

"I'm not a doctor," Clay corrected.

He made coffee and warmed up cornbread given them by the Boxers, along with beans. He was glad to see Wes eating and acting more alert.

After they ate, Carmody's curiosity about Katherine continued.

"Were you born in Kansas?" the gunman asked.

"Yes. My mother died when I was small. I stayed with an aunt in Kansas. When she died, I left finishing school and came west to be with my brothers. I traveled with an officer and his wife to Camp Grant. Sid met me there."

"How many brothers do you have?" Carmody asked.

"Just two. Sid was the oldest. Now there's only Jacob."

She took a moment to explain to Carmody what had happened to Sid. Tears filled her eyes. She was quiet for a while.

"Castle Creek is beautiful," she said, at length. "The Wileys have the biggest ranch, but it's more prairie than grassland. My brothers have the best land. Everyone wants it because there's a river running right through it. I'm afraid there may be a war before it's over."

"Ought to be some way to live in peace," Clay said.

She looked up from her coffee, studying him a moment. Then she leaned back on the rocks, shaking her head.

"Men would rather fight."

"Not true."

"I grew up in Kansas, remember? The war's been over twelve years, but they won't let it be."

Carmody smiled, leaning back on his saddle. Wes had already curled up in his blankets, sound asleep.

Clay poured himself some more coffee. Katherine declined a refill, but studied Clay a moment.

"You look better without a beard. Almost handsome," she said. "Where did you get the scar?"

"An Apache knife, that's all."

"I never thought Clay Darringer was so modest," Carmody said.

Clay ignored the gunman's sneer. "I'll take first watch," he decided.

Katherine drew her blankets around her and lay close to the fire, her red hair glistening in the light as she closed her eyes.

Both men sat looking at her. Clay, considering Carmody's obviously dishonorable thoughts, knew he had to make sure she was safe when he left.

He pulled on his leather coat. Taking his Winchester and blanket, he went to the head of the hollow where the horses were tethered. It was dark and cold and silent.

While watching the surrounding terrain, he also kept an eye on the campfire. Katherine was asleep. Carmody had at last turned into his blankets, his head on his saddle and hat over his face, six-gun in his hand.

Clay knew about the gunman from Wyoming. A killer of men, Carmody was for hire to the highest bidder and didn't mind changing sides.

An hour before dawn, dozing off and on, Clay heard the yip of the coyote again. Rising slowly, he listened carefully. An answering yip followed. They were closer this time.

Moving silently back into the hollow, he knelt by Katherine where she lay in her blankets. He put his hand on her mouth. She stared at him fearfully.

He awakened Carmody and Wes.

Sitting up, she watched them make their beds with rocks in the blankets. With dismay, she obeyed Clay by slipping back into her own bedding, holding his Colt in both hands, hammer back. She and Wes would be the bait—she and her flaming red hair. Her eyes were round and wild as she lay down.

Carmody gave Wes a six-gun to keep under his blankets, then slipped back into the rocks. Clay moved back behind a boulder, kneeling with the Winchester repeater cocked and ready. The only sound was the crackling fire. He had learned long ago it was a myth that Indians would not fight in the dark.

He could hear his own breathing. He listened for the horses to make a nervous sound. Instead, there was only silence.

Suddenly, a hundred and seventy pounds of fury landed on him. The Apache knife slid right by his throat as Clay spun under the weight. He struggled, fighting furiously. They clawed at each other, the Winchester falling into the grass.

He slammed his fist in the Apache's face, throwing him against the rocks and landing on him. They fought for the knife, still in the red man's hand. Both were panting for breath, groaning with effort.

The sudden explosion of a gunshot from the camp rang out, and Clay panicked, fearful for Katherine. With a great burst of power, he gripped the Apache's hand, turning the knife toward the man's chest. Furious black eyes gleamed back at him in the moonlight.

Abruptly, the knife went into the Apache's heart.

Still fighting, the renegade gasped and crumpled, dying while Clay still held him. Taking a deep breath, Clay released him and spun about, grabbing his Winchester and rushing into the hollow.

Wes was staggering out of his blankets.

The other Apache lay across Katherine. She was nearly hysterical, trying to sit up under him, both hands on the Colt. Her face drained of color, she stared up at Clay. She looked so small, so terrified, that he felt a pain in his gut.

Carmody had shot her assailant, then slipped into the night, and was now returning. He shook his head as he holstered his six-gun and helped Clay drag the dead Apache away from her and off into the rocks. It was then they realized she had also shot her attacker, square in the chest.

Wes knelt at her side, calming her.

"I figure there was just two," Carmody said.

"You don't mind if I take a look," Clay murmured.

Carmody shook his head, kneeling by Katherine and Wes.

Eyes wild, she finally lowered the weapon as Clay turned away to scout the area, rifle in one hand, his knife in the other. Daylight was easing the shadows as he moved through boulders and brush, watching and waiting. There was no response to his movements. He read sign in the early light.

Satisfied at last that there had been only two Apaches, he returned to camp and set his rifle aside. He knelt to force the Colt from Katherine's tight grip, then holstered it.

She was shaking all over, wrapping her arms about herself. Her lips were quivering, her eyes still wild.

"We can eat first or break camp," he said.

"I don't want to stay here," she whispered, frantic.

He nodded, pausing on one knee to look at her. Her green eyes were filling with tears. He understood. She had shot two men in a matter of days. The move from finishing school to the frontier had been too sudden.

He took her hand, pulling her to her feet. Her fingers were small and cold. He stood looking at her distress, not realizing he still held her hand.

"She's all right now," Carmody said.

Clay quickly released her hand and turned to kick dirt in the fire, deciding they would move out of the area and then camp for breakfast.

An hour later, they were again settled down by a campfire, this time in the rocks on a knoll, shaded by two cottonwoods.

After they had breakfast, the conversation turned to the Army and the San Carlos Reservation. Clay told them about John Clum.

"He did good things for the Apache but resigned last summer. After General Crook left, nothing had gone right."

"I know the Apache," Wes said. "I used to have a lot of fun with a couple Chiricahua boys my age, before they were sent to San Carlos. They like to play games, especially horse racing. But when they fight, I guess they got a reason."

"They got plenty of reason," Clay said. "It's their country."

"Do you have any other family?" Katherine asked the boy.

"An uncle, back East somewhere," Wes replied. "But maybe I can find a job in Castle Creek."

"My brother has a ranch there," Katherine told him. "He may have a job for you. Can you work cattle?"

"I can learn," the boy said. "You know, Doc, I feel better already."

"Just take it easy. And I'm not a doctor," Clay reminded him.

"You're one of them gunfighters," Wes said.

"One of *those* gunfighters," Katherine corrected.

"Both of you had best visit the local law," Clay added. "As soon as you get to town."

"That would be the sheriff," Wes said. "He ain't too friendly."

"*Isn't* too friendly," Katherine said.

Wes made a face that let them know he wasn't used to being corrected, especially by a woman. Katherine merely smiled as she refilled the boy's plate.

When they had finished eating, they broke camp and saddled their mounts. Carmody polished his silver-laden saddle.

Mounted once more, they rode on through the hills.

Red rocks were giving way to sand-colored boulders. Vegetation was heavier and green. The sky was clear, pale blue. The air was thinner and colder.

On a high hill in the late afternoon, they reined up in a grove of golden aspen to view the town sprawled at the southern entrance to the vast, wooded valley. Clay had been here once with the Army. He remembered the big creek running just east of town, south toward the endless prairie.

Yellow and red ridges circled most of the rolling valley on the far north. The wooded, mostly flat country on the east side, where they were riding, was grassy but with sandy soil.

In the west, the hills rolled gently higher. Beyond

was the beginning of forested, snow-crested mountains.

"Apache Peaks," Clay said.

Overhead, a great golden eagle circled, then sped away toward the nearby cottonwoods. There was no wind. The world was silent, the view breathtaking.

At length, Katherine spoke.

"If this is the east side, we're on Wiley land. Our place is on the west side, in the hill country. There's a large grove of aspens on the first hill, in the shape of a cross. A few miles farther is the river, which runs south to the prairie, where it sort of disappears as it goes along."

They sat a long while, admiring the view.

In the stillness, Clay stiffened at the sound of a repeating rifle being cocked. He knew it was pointed at his back.

Chapter Three

T here on the ridge, stiff in the saddle, Clay, Carmody, Katherine, and Wes didn't move. Their faces were to the sun, which was low in the western sky. Below was the prairie entrance to the valley. Behind them was a rifle.

"Reach," a man's voice said.

Wes and Carmody lifted their hands. Katherine didn't move.

Clay slowly turned his horse around, his right hand resting on the pommel, not far from his holster. Wes, Carmody, and Katherine also began to turn their mounts. Carmody, seeing that Clay wasn't reaching, lowered his own hands. So did Wes.

Facing them were three men. The obvious leader was a crass-looking, bearded man in his fifties. In his hands was a leveled Winchester repeater.

"I'm Riggs, foreman of the Wiley ranch," he said. "You're all trespassing."

"Our folks was murdered," Wes replied. "Mr. Darringer's just seein' us to Castle Creek."

"Darringer?" Riggs queried.

"Clay Darringer," Wes said.

There was a long silence as Riggs and the two cow-hands digested this news. The foreman cast his beady eyes on Clay, looking him over.

One of the hands was lean and sloppy in the saddle. He had a clean-cut, almost boyish face, but his dark eyes were searing. And he was looking over Katherine rather well.

In turn, she was staring back at him, her face white.

"What's a gunfighter doin' in Castle Creek?" Riggs grunted.

"He's helping us," Wes said, rising tall in the saddle. "So is Mr. Carmody."

Riggs and his men reacted. It wasn't surprise, Clay decided. Maybe it was recognition.

After a moment, Riggs shrugged. "Well, you get on your way. I'll be reportin' this to Mr. Wiley."

"And Sheb Wiley?" Katherine asked.

Riggs glared at her. "What about Sheb?"

"Is he on the ranch?" she persisted.

"Just get on your way," Riggs responded.

"Is he dead?" she asked.

"You ask too many questions," Riggs snapped. "Woman oughta know her place."

"Don't talk to her like that," Wes snapped.

"And you, Darringer," Riggs said, ignoring the boy, "ain't you got a tongue?"

"He talks with his shootin' iron," Wes warned, "so you'd better back off."

"Riggs," the sloppy cowhand said, grinning, "I think he's right. And, Miss Turner, maybe you don't remember me. My name's Tuck Wiley."

"I remember," she muttered, her nose tipped upward.

"Maybe I'll come callin'," Tuck said.

"No, you won't," she said coolly.

Tuck only laughed. "Women always say no when they mean maybe."

Katherine was pale but stiff in the saddle.

Riggs was glaring at Clay's steel-gray eyes. The gunfighter's silence was unnerving the foreman. He lowered his rifle and spun his horse about, the young cowhand following as he rode off through the trees. The grinning Tuck Wiley took another hungry look at Katherine before following the others.

When they were gone, Clay drew a deep breath.

"Clay," Wes said, "you got him without firing a shot."

"Remarkable," Carmody added, smiling with a sneer.

Clay grimaced as he led the way down the ridge trail, refusing to look at Katherine or Wes. He smelled plenty of trouble with them around.

As for Carmody, the time would soon come to learn why the gunman was riding to Castle Creek. He was obviously on hire by someone.

As Clay and his companions rode down into the valley, Riggs and the other two men reined up in the woods. The foreman leaned on his saddle, rubbing his grizzly chin.

"Now why do you suppose she was so interested in Sheb?"

"Don't you worry about it," Tuck said.

"She was mighty upset about somethin'," Riggs added.

"I'll talk to Sheb," Tuck promised. "You fellas got work to do. But just in case, you'd better make sure none of the men let on that Sheb's back."

"Most don't even know it," Riggs said. "Sheb got back late last night. Them Texas boys that come in with 'im, they bunked out in the barn and ain't mixed with the men. And the herd's still a ways out."

Leaving the foreman and young cowhand behind, Tuck rode on back to the ranch. It was nearly dark. The big, rambling house was set at the foot of a great rocky peak. Ignoring the bunkhouse and corrals to the right, Tuck rode up to the house and dismounted.

Inside, he found his father busy with the books, seated in a leather chair in the warmth of the hearth. Tuck didn't bother him, moving instead up the stairs to look for Sheb.

His older brother had just gotten out of bed after sleeping all day. Grinning, Tuck sat backward on a chair, resting his arms and chin on the curved back frame. Both men had boyish faces, dark dangerous eyes, and foolish grins.

"What's the matter with you?" Sheb asked.

"Tell me what kind of trouble you got into in Texas."

"No trouble."

"But them four Texas boys you hired on with the herd, ain't they a bit too wild for cowhands?"

"What's eatin' you?" Sheb grunted, rubbing his wiry chin. He stood up and walked to the basin, bending over to wash his face.

"And I seen you out in the corral last night when you rode in with one of them bad Shanty Wells boys."

Drying his face, Sheb was getting annoyed. "Just spell it out, Tuck."

"Well, you always keep things to yourself, so I was just wonderin' if I oughta tell you what I know."

"All right, Tuck, what the devil do you know?"

"You remember a couple years ago when Katherine Turner was out here?"

Sheb's boyish face darkened. He turned his back.

"What about it?" Sheb grunted.

"Well, she's back, and askin' about you."

Sheb's body turned to stone. He couldn't move for a long, worried moment. Cold sweat covered his face. Again, he used the towel. He didn't turn around as he pretended to wash his hands.

"She sure is pretty," Tuck said. " 'Course you and me, we ain't educated. Maybe she'd rather have our little brother Thad, now that he's goin' to be a gentleman."

Sheb busied himself getting dressed and strapping on his six-gun, refusing to look at his younger brother. Tuck continued to needle him.

"But then maybe she's got a yen for you, Sheb."

"I'm goin' huntin' for a few days. You just tell Riggs to make sure the hands don't tell anyone they saw me."

"What about your Texas boys?"

"You just tell 'em what you told me. I've already paid 'em off."

"Sure there's nothin' you wanta tell me?"

"For once," Sheb grunted, "I wish you'd do what I asked."

"Well, then, I ain't tellin' you my secrets nohow."

Sheb pulled down his wool-lined leather coat and draped it over his arm. He picked up his Winchester repeater.

Tuck just grinned, stepping aside for Sheb, who led the way into the hallway and down the stairs. Sheb was a little taller and stronger, as well as a lot smarter, but Tuck could easily rout him.

Their father, Tate, a tall, erect man with a long face and square jaw, looked up from his work. His eyes were as dark as theirs, but without the searing penetration. A former military officer, he still looked as if he were in uniform.

On the table next to him was a picture of their mother, and another print of Thad in uniform.

Pencil in hand, he waved to them to join him. Reluctantly, his sons approached.

"Sheb," he said gruffly, "I can't figure out these books. Your writing's like hen scratch."

"Don't matter none," Sheb replied. "It all balances."

"Well," Tate said, closing the ledgers, "I didn't see you last night when you got back. Why don't you sit here by the fire and tell me about the drive? It's suppertime, anyhow."

"I got somethin' to do," Sheb said.

"Sheb's goin' huntin'," Tuck added, grinning.

"Why?" Tate asked, surprised.

" 'Counta I got some thinkin' to do," Sheb said grimly.

"And he don't want anyone to know he's back," Tuck put in.

"What've you been up to?" Tate asked his older son.

"Can't talk now, Pa," Sheb said.

Tate sat straight in his chair, watching Sheb head out the door and slam it behind him. He turned and looked at the grinning Tuck.

"Are you going to tell me what's going on?" Tate demanded.

"Can't, Pa. I don't know anything. Except that Katherine Turner's back. And Sheb's hidin' out."

"You saw her?"

"Ridin' in with some gunfighters. Fella named Clay Darringer, and that Carmody."

"Have you been drinking?"

"No, Pa, just havin' a little fun."

Tate's face darkened. He watched his younger son head for the door. Settling back in his leather chair, he stared at the wild flames eating the wood.

While Tate pondered the news, the newcomers were riding in the moonlight toward Castle Creek. They could see the lights of the town as they crossed the shallow stream.

Carmody suddenly tipped his hat to Katherine and nodded to Clay, smiling his farewell. Then he set his heels to his bay and rode at a gallop toward the town, leaving them behind.

Clay was glad to see him go. He rode slowly, with Katherine and Wes keeping pace. The silence between the three of them was awareness of their friendship coming to an end.

Just south of town, Clay suddenly reined up. "You'll be safe now."

"You can't leave us like this," Katherine said. "What if the sheriff isn't there? And how will I get to my brother's ranch?"

"Maybe Mr. Carmody would help," Wes said.

"Stay away from him," Clay warned.

He reached into his pocket and pulled out some gold coins, tossing them to Wes. The boy caught them and stared at the way they gleamed in his hand.

"Get some rooms for the night," Clay told him.

"But it's Saturday night," Katherine protested. "It could be dangerous in town. And that Tuck Wiley will be running back to his father. They may come after me."

"Just tell the sheriff what you know," Clay said.

"At least you could see me to the ranch," Katherine countered.

"I came three days out of my way as it is," Clay replied.

"Let him go," Wes said to her. "I'll take care o' you."

Clay drew a deep breath. Darringers were always getting into the middle of someone else's trouble. It was a family failing.

Maybe he could stay the night at least, see that they had safe rooms and no one bothered them. He could look around town for some of her father's hands and see to it that they took her home in the morning.

"I'll go along," Clay said, "but just to see that you

get settled. I'll talk to the sheriff. Then I'll be on my way."

Katherine smiled her gratitude. Moonlight was sprinkled in her red hair. He avoided looking at her.

The first building was the livery, on the left side of the street. It was a huge old barn, backed by corrals with a few horses and mules. The big doors in front were wide open. Three men were walking out and heading up the street. One was a tall, heavyset man with a rifle.

There was no sign of Carmody or his horse.

Clay rode into the livery first and dismounted. The owner was a short, fat man with gray hair. He gave them stalls and told them the best hotel was the only hotel, the Castle.

"We got us a pretty good town," the man said. "And if you ride up through the valley to the rim, you'll see why it's called Castle Creek. Got some old Indian dwellings."

After taking care of their mounts, Clay and his companions left the livery. Wes was carrying Katherine's carpetbag. Clay had his bedroll and saddlebags, along with his Winchester, having left his possibles in the stall.

It was moon bright. The single street ran north between two rows of buildings, all of timber.

At this end of town, there were six saloons, three on each side, their light filtering into the street. Laughter and music came from two of them. A woman was singing along with an out-of-tune piano. Horses were tied at the railings, heads down. Wagons were further up the street.

After the saloons, they passed stores on either side. Some were for miners. Most were for ranchers and farmers. Windows displayed twenty-dollar boots and fancy ladies' hats.

The boardwalks were in better condition as they continued north. They passed a newspaper office, a barber and undertaker, and a gunsmith. Over the mercantile, there was a sign for the doctor's office. Lamps hung from poles burned somberly about every fifty feet along the boardwalk.

Houses were set back to the west. The Castle Hotel was a big rambling building on the right. It had a wide porch and a veranda around the second floor. Bright lights inside reached the boardwalk.

Across the street from the hotel was the sheriff's office, a streak of light at each front window.

"Get yourselves a couple of rooms," Clay said. "I'll go talk to the sheriff. You can see him tomorrow."

"Why not now?" Katherine asked.

"Because I said so," Clay replied, annoyed.

She was startled, her green eyes flashing. She gave Clay a stern look that slowly softened. Then she smiled and turned to go up the hotel steps.

Clay was irritated by her reaction. She was assuming he was taking charge, and he didn't want that.

"I'll be gone come morning," Clay said.

She paused, turning to look down at him. The lights behind her framed her nice figure and cast a red glow in her hair. Her voice was hushed.

"Then thank you, Clay Darringer. I'll miss you."

She spun on her heel and went inside. Wes stood

near Clay for a moment, his left hand still gripping her carpetbag. Then he extended his right.

"Thanks, Mr. Darringer."

"Clay. How about stashing my gear with the clerk?"

The boy shook his hand, took Clay's gear, and went up the steps, disappearing inside the hotel.

Clay swallowed hard. He had become attached to them. All the more reason to get the heck out of town. But first he would have a word with the sheriff. He took up his Winchester and crossed the street.

The sheriff's office was a big room about twenty feet square. The two front windows had board covers. The side walls had rifle slots. A pot-bellied stove and bunk were on the right, the desk and bulletin board on the left.

The two cells in the back were empty.

Behind the big wooden desk sat a big hard man. He was solid everything, muscle, energy, and composure. His face was like stone, carved and strong. His blue eyes were nearly white, like his hair. He was probably fifty. His wide mouth was set in a grimace as he looked up from his meal.

"I'm Sheriff Cox. What can I do for you?"

"I'm Clay Darringer."

The sheriff almost choked on his food. He swallowed hard, then downed some coffee. He leaned back in his chair, glaring at Clay. He obviously didn't like gunfighters in his town.

"You still wanted, Darringer?"

"No, I have a pardon," Clay said, drawing it from inside his shirt. The parchment was sweaty and wrinkled, but he handed it to Cox to review. After a moment, the lawman handed it back.

"So a little Texas chivalry got you in trouble."

"Something like that," Clay said, returning his pardon to his secret pocket.

"And what are you doing here?"

"I brought in two young people," Clay said as he sat down. "One is Wes Barnes. The Army was chasing Apaches when they found his family murdered. Probably by Victorio. He was thrown when they shot his horse, but he'll be all right."

"I've seen the boy in town."

"The other is Katherine Turner. Her brother Sid and two cowhands were murdered by outlaws in Bravo Canyon a few days south. She was left for dead. Now she'd like to get to her brother's ranch. I thought I'd see if any of his hands are in town. They could look after her."

"Well, I reckon her troubles ain't over. Her brother Jacob was shot up pretty bad in an ambush about two weeks ago. He's out to the ranch now, laid up."

Clay digested this before speaking.

"The Wileys have anything to do with it?"

"Why're you askin'?" Cox grunted.

"Miss Turner shot one of the killers before he clubbed her down. She said it was Sheb Wiley."

"Well, Sheb's been gone to Texas for a few months, but that don't prove nothin'."

"Except he wasn't here to shoot Jacob, so who you figure done that?" Clay asked.

"I don't know, but the Wileys ain't the only ones

wantin' that land. A few of the other ranchers been gettin' mighty fidgety. Like the Renshaws."

"This all cattle country?"

"Got a pig and chicken farm up the end of the valley. A couple others raisin' corn, I reckon. And a sawmill."

"I was told that Turner's got a river on his place."

"Sure has," Cox replied. "With its own little valley. Prettiest spot you ever saw."

Clay leaned back in his chair. Things were getting too complicated.

"You might find some Turner hands down at the first saloon on this side of the street," the lawman said. "Are you going to be hanging around?"

"Nope."

"Just as well. The Wileys are a mean bunch, but they've been quiet about it. You might stir things up."

"You call ambush bein' quiet?"

"Now there ain't no proof the Wileys shot Jacob," the lawman said. "Every rancher but Turner has got to keep his herd down so water and grass will last through the dry season. That don't sit well with any of 'em."

Clay shrugged and stood up slowly. He met the sheriff's gaze, knowing he was being studied in depth.

"One thing you oughta know," Clay said. "Carmody's in town."

"Jace Carmody?"

"That's him."

The lawman grimaced. "So I got two of you on my hands."

"Don't be puttin' my name with his," Clay said.

"Well, whether you're the same brand or not, he's going to be testin' you, sooner or later."

Turning, Clay walked toward the door, just as it was thrust open. Katherine was hurrying inside, her face so white that her freckles looked as red as her hair.

"Sheriff, I just heard about my brother Jacob," she said, frantic. "You've got to take me to the ranch tonight."

"Now, hold on," the lawman protested. "I can't leave town on a Saturday night. Besides, your brother's resting all right. Just see Doc Miller tomorrow. His office is over the mercantile. He'll set your mind at ease."

"But I want to see Jacob now," she said.

"Well, Clay, here, he was going to see if any of your hands are in town."

"I'll go with you," she told Clay.

"Not a chance," Clay said firmly.

She pouted her lips, glaring at him. After a long consideration of his grim response, she relaxed slightly.

"All right," she relented, "but promise you'll come to the hotel right after. I'll wait in the lobby. And, Sheriff, you have to arrest Sheb Wiley for killing my brother Sid. And when are you going to catch the men that shot Jacob?"

The lawman leaned back, studying this wisp of a beautiful woman with the fearless challenge.

She waited for the lawman to answer. When he didn't, she bit her lip in her frustration and helplessness. She spun on her heel, charging for the door. On the way out, she paused, turning to look at Clay.

"I'll be waiting," she said.

When she was gone, the door closing behind her, the lawman drew a deep breath, leaning back in his chair. Suddenly, he grinned. "What a woman."

"Young enough to be your daughter," Clay pointed out.

"But not so young for you, eh?"

"I'm heading for California," Clay said, turning to go outside, into the cool night.

He closed the door and looked up and down the empty street. Horses and mules stood with heads down. A wagon was in front of the mercantile. Music came from the first saloon on the hotel side of the street.

Clay walked to the first saloon on the sheriff's side, pausing at the swinging doors to view the quiet, smoky interior.

About twenty men lounged about, playing cards or just chewing the fat. On the left, the bartender was busy arguing with an old hand whose hair and handlebar mustache were white as snow.

Clay entered. The men glanced at him curiously as he walked to the bar. He leaned on the shining walnut and looked directly at the bartender, a bald and chubby man.

"I'm looking for some Turner hands," Clay said.

"What for?" the barkeep asked.

"To escort Katherine Turner to the ranch."

The white-haired man stiffened. His weathered face was lined from years in the saddle. He was short and stocky. His pale blue eyes narrowed as he took Clay's measure.

"I'm Hal Perkins, foreman at the Turner ranch."

"I'd think you'd be up there, keeping an eye on things," Clay said.

Perkins straightened, taking offense. "I left five hands at the house up there, and I don't take kindly to insults."

"Miss Turner's waitin' in the hotel lobby," Clay said.

"Ain't safe to ride her up there tonight," Perkins replied. "I got three men in here, but I figure she can wait."

"Why don't you tell her that?" Clay suggested.

Perkins looked mighty irritated. Finally, he downed his drink and walked with Clay toward the door as he glanced at his men. The hands sat quiet, watching their foreman leave with the stranger.

It was a cold night. The sky was sprinkled with stars and a pale moon. As Clay and Perkins walked along the dark, deserted boardwalk, the foreman glared sideways at him.

"Who are you, anyway?"

"Clay Darringer."

"What's the likes of you got to do with Miss Turner?"

"Found her a few days south. Her brother Sid and two men were killed. She's pretty certain one of the killers was Sheb Wiley."

"Dadburn it," Perkins muttered. "I tell you, Darringer, this valley's going to bust wide open. Maybe it's just as well you're here, dependin' what side you're on, that is."

"I'm heading west," Clay said.

"You tellin' me you're not for hire?"

"Never was."

Perkins glared at him, not convinced.

"Well, word is, someone sent for some fancy gun," the foreman said. "I figured it was you."

Clay shook his head. "No, but Carmody's in town."

"Blast. He's a bad one."

They were in front of the gunsmith now, not quite to the sheriff's office. They cut across toward the hotel at an angle. Lamps hanging in the establishment's open porch were beckoning to them. The street was dry and dusty.

As they neared the pale lights of the hotel, a rifle barked in the stillness, a bullet singing by Clay and striking Perkins in the right foot. The foreman yelped.

Clay spun, six-gun in hand. Perkins hopped crazily toward the porch, Clay following. Again the rifle barked, the bullet striking Perkins's right leg below the knee. The foreman yelped again and danced about.

This time, Clay had seen the flash of light from an alley between the last store and first saloon on the hotel side of the street. He shoved Perkins toward the porch. The man fell and crawled up the steps.

Cox came charging out of his office, rifle in hand. The street was silent but for his running steps.

Clay had moved into the shadows next to the hotel.

The lawman joined him, while Perkins was dragged inside by two men who had run out to help.

The Turner hands and others had come out of all the saloons but one. Sensing trouble, they were backing inside again. No faces had appeared at the first saloon on the hotel side of the street.

"Came from the alley, this side of that first saloon," Clay said, pointing with his Colt.

"Follow me," Cox told him.

Clay didn't hesitate. He moved behind the sheriff as they made their way in the dark between the hotel and the barber's.

They stopped, listening and waiting. There were no running feet, no hoofbeats. The dirt muffled their footsteps as they moved carefully past the stores and toward the alley in question. Peering into the space, they saw nothing but some boxes and a broken wheel.

"Whoever it was," Cox said quietly, "is probably still inside. This place is a Wiley hangout. There's a back door."

"I'll take the front."

"No, you stay in back."

Clay shrugged, watching the lawman move along the street. When Cox was out of sight, Clay walked through mud where water had been discarded in the alley. Pausing at the open door at the back of the saloon, he scraped his boots on the porch. The mud was red in the pale lamplight.

As he entered the back storeroom, he heard piano music and the murmur of talk, but no laughter.

He walked past the boxes and barrels, moving into a short, dark hallway that opened to the saloon. He quietly moved to the last step, where he could not be seen.

Twenty-two men were seated around the tables. They appeared to be cowhands, hats pushed back on their heads, legs sprawled. Some wore sidearms. Most were playing cards. A few looked mean as sin. The bar and piano were to Clay's left, and he couldn't see them from where he stood.

Sheriff Cox entered through the swinging doors, rifle slanted at his side. Some of the men turned their heads to look at him.

One man, seated against the wall, was busy peering into his hand of cards. He was leaning forward, concentrating. A big, chunky man with a large nose and a white scar on his chin, he had strong hands and a narrowed mouth. At his left hip, a six-gun was holstered. There was no sign of the rifle Clay had seen him carrying from the livery just an hour before.

But the man's boots were caked with red mud.

Cox looked around the room as he moved to put his back to the wall. The piano music had stopped, and the player was hurrying out the front entrance. Gradually, other men nervously stood up and left the saloon. The only men remaining were the four at the table with the big-nosed man.

The lawman concentrated on that table.

"Anyone see a man with a rifle?" he asked.

The five men shrugged. Clay moved into the light.

"What about you, Thatcher?" the lawman persisted.

The big-nosed man looked up with a grimace. "I got no rifle."

"But he has muddy boots," Clay said. "Red mud, from the alley."

"Butt out, mister," Thatcher growled.

"His name is Clay Darringer," the lawman said.

Suddenly, the other four men jerked their chairs back, got to their feet, and backed away toward the bar, working their way around to the door.

Thatcher glared at their departure. The doors swung freely behind them as they hurried into the street.

"Stand up, Thatcher," the lawman ordered, leveling his rifle.

Slowly, the big man got to his feet. "You got nothin' on me. A lot of men come in the back way, just like I did."

"No one else had red mud on their boots," Clay pointed out.

"Don't prove nothin'," the big man said.

"Check behind the bar," the lawman told Clay.

Moving back and to the left, Clay reached the bar, noticing that the bartender had also disappeared. He walked behind the long walnut frame. Bottles and glasses were stacked in front of the large mirror. Under the bar top, he found a shotgun, as usual, but no rifle.

He walked to the other back door, finding that it opened to the next alley. There was no sign of the rifle. Maybe the bartender had taken it.

"Only two sets of boots came out of the mud in that alley," Clay said. "Mine and a man with big feet. Let's see if his boots fit the prints."

"I ain't movin' one inch," Thatcher said.

Cox shoved his rifle into the man's belly. "Move."

With a grunt, Thatcher turned, walking toward the back entrance, the others following with a lantern. Outside in the moonlight, Cox ordered the man to place his boot inside the unidentified print. It was a good match.

"Don't prove nothin'," Thatcher said.

"It's enough to lock you up," Cox told him. "Drop that gun belt with your left hand."

Thatcher slowly unbuckled and dropped his gun belt. He looked plenty mean. Cox marched the man back into the saloon, Clay following with the man's weapon.

"You can't prove nothin'," Thatcher said.

"Maybe not," Cox agreed, "but we'll let the circuit judge decide. He'll be here about next Friday."

Thatcher growled. "I'll be out long before that."

"You still working for Wiley?" Cox asked him.

"They told me a couple of days ago that I had a week to draw my pay and move on. But that don't bother me none."

Cox marched the man into the empty street and across toward the jail. Clay followed, covering the lawman's back. They reached the boardwalk and moved toward the jailhouse.

Inside, Cox turned up the lamps before locking the big man in the left-hand cell. He returned the keys to his desk. Then he looked at Clay.

"Thanks," the lawman said.

"We should check on Perkins."

Cox nodded. He and Clay went outside, closing the

door to the office and walking across the empty street. They carefully glanced in all directions, looking for signs of more trouble. It was dark and silent.

Clay led the way up the steps and onto the porch. They entered the hotel lobby. Lamps were burning brightly. The hotel was nicely decorated with green drapes and a lush green rug. The furniture was soft, sprinkled with white and green.

To the left, a bespectacled little man was standing behind the desk. To the right, a short, bald doctor was busy at the sofa, working on Perkins's right leg and foot. Two men who appeared to be merchants were assisting. It was they who had pulled Perkins into the hotel.

Standing nearby were Katherine and Wes.

"You get him?" Wes asked.

"We figure it was Thatcher," the lawman said. "I got him locked up."

The doctor straightened to look at Cox. "All right if I take Perkins to my office now?"

"Go ahead," Cox said. "I'll be right behind you."

Perkins sat up, his right leg and foot wrapped with a bandage already soaked with blood. He looked at Katherine, who came forward.

"Sorry, Miss Turner," Perkins said, "but I still figure to get you to the ranch tomorrow."

"You'd better think about that," Cox cautioned. "Might be safer in town."

"Perkins isn't going anywhere," the doctor cut in. "There's still a bullet in there. And he'll have to keep it elevated a couple of days."

"But I have to go to the ranch," Katherine said.

The two merchants lifted Perkins and helped him hobble out on his good leg. The doctor and Cox walked along behind him. The others watched until they were outside.

Katherine looked less sure of herself than before. She clasped her hands together at her waist. She looked pale, her freckles peach-colored. The bruise on her forehead was barely visible now.

Wes, however, was grim. "Mr. Darringer, we'd sure like to hire you."

"I'm movin' on," Clay said.

"And who's going to help Miss Turner?" Wes asked. "A bunch of cowhands? Even the foreman's shot up."

Clay looked at the stress on Katherine's face. Gone was the outspoken challenge. There was only powerless frustration and pain in her gaze.

A helpless woman was too much for Clay. He wanted to turn and head for the door. Yet he hesitated. She had lost her parents long ago and had witnessed the death of one of her brothers. She had nearly died. Now her brother Jacob was laid up. Her foreman was wounded.

That left a few cowhands, Wes, and a busy lawman to help her.

"Well?" Wes persisted.

"It's all right, Wes," Katherine said. "Mr. Darringer doesn't want to stay."

"Well, maybe we can hire Mr. Carmody," Wes suggested.

She turned her back to them, as if to hide her tears.

That was all Clay could handle. He swallowed hard.

"All right," he said. "I'll stay until Jacob is back on his feet."

He saw her stiffen as if choked on her emotions. Slowly, she turned. Tears were trickling down her pretty face.

"Thank you," she whispered.

"I'll meet you at breakfast, right after sunup," he said, nodding toward the hotel dining room in the rear. "Lock your door."

She nodded, watching him as he turned away.

Feeling her gaze following him, he hurried toward the door. Grim, disgusted with himself, he went outside.

Pausing on the boardwalk, he glanced toward the sheriff's office, where lights burned low. Cox was going to have his hands full with Thatcher and the Wileys. Clay felt a need to help the lawman.

But Clay also knew he couldn't abandon Katherine.

Even if it meant a bullet in his back.

Chapter Four

*L*ate that Saturday night, Clay went to the doctor's office above the mercantile. It was a series of small rooms. In the first, he found the medic washing his hands. Doctor Amos Miller was very business-like.

"I'm Clay Darringer."

"I know who you are, son."

"I'd like to see Perkins."

"He's in there now with his men. Go ahead."

"Is his leg all right?" Clay asked.

"Got the bullet out, if that's what you mean."

"Any internal hemorrhaging?"

Miller glanced at him curiously. "No, and what do you know about it?"

"Studied for a year with a surgeon."

"I could use some help," the doctor said. "I can't pay much, but—"

"No, thanks," Clay told him. "I made my peace with that a long time ago."

"And took up the gun?"

Clay shrugged and moved past him.

"I lost my only son 'counta the gun," the doctor

said, "just one year ago. He and Howie Renshaw shot it out over cards. They claimed it was a fair fight, even though my son had been drinking too much, but it weren't right for Howie to gut-shoot him."

Clay paused, waiting, but the doctor said no more. Then Clay went on to the back room where Perkins was lying on a tall bed, his right leg up on pillows. Sitting around, hats pushed back, were three young cowhands, faces fresh and clean-shaven.

"Boys, this is Clay Darringer," Perkins said.

The men introduced themselves, shook Clay's hand, and then went to the doorway, pausing as Clay spoke.

"I'll be escortin' Miss Turner out to the ranch in the morning. I'd be obliged if you'd be at the hotel shortly after sunup."

They nodded agreement and left.

"Good boys," Perkins said, "but mighty young."

"What about you? Can you be moved?" Clay asked.

"Doc wants me here a couple of days. Have some of the boys come for me with a wagon."

Clay sat down in one of the chairs, pushing his hat back.

Perkins studied him. "Seems to me you forgot about California."

"Mighty hard to ride out," Clay said. "You know she isn't safe anywhere."

Perkins nodded. "I don't know what to do about it."

"Would the ranch withstand an attack?"

"Well, it's got walls around the house from days

when they was fightin' Injuns, but the courtyard's big and hard to cover. Then they built a second story on the house, so it's up higher than the walls. I don't know, Darringer. They shot Jacob one night when he was leaving town. So far, nobody's come near the house."

"You figure it's the Wileys?"

"Not sure, but ole Wiley always talked like he'd do anything to have a place as big as the King Ranch in Texas."

"That's a tall order," Clay said.

"Anyhow, the Wileys and Renshaws both tried to buy the Turners out. The smaller ranchers were gettin' money together to do the same thing, but the brothers wouldn't sell."

"But there's a lot of unsettled land in this country," Clay said. "Why is this particular valley so important?"

"Well, for one thing, railroad's gonna cross south of here," Perkins said. "And the Territory's gettin' crowded. Good grass on a big scale ain't that easy to find nowadays, especially with water runnin' through it."

Clay stood up slowly, pulling his hat back to his brow.

"Take care of her," Perkins said.

Clay shook his hand and went to the door.

"You know," Perkins added, "whoever's doin' it, they're gonna try to get her and Jacob, one way or another. They got no other kin. That might put the place up for grabs."

Clay nodded and went back into the front office.

The doctor, who was folding bandages, paused to look at him.

"Watch yourself," Dr. Miller said.

"Thanks."

Clay left and went onto the landing, standing in the dark and looking down at the quiet street. Men who only fought from ambush were foreign to him.

He understood the Apache. They were ingenious, often hiding under the dirt to ambush their prey, but they still fought to the death, face-to-face. Clay had met other men in gunfights. He had fought in open range wars. But he just didn't understand men like these killers.

He went down the creaky steps to the boardwalk, then back to the jailhouse. The door was locked. He tapped lightly with his fist.

A shuttered window opened a crack to his right. Then the door opened and Cox came outside into the cold.

"We're leaving after breakfast," Clay said. "I'm taking her to the ranch."

"Figured you would."

"What about you? It's not going to be any picnic when whoever hired Thatcher tries to break him out."

"I ain't worried," Cox said. "Of course, I would have liked you to stick around."

"Well, I had to choose between you and Miss Turner."

"I reckon she's prettier, all right."

Clay grinned, then sobered. He shook the man's hand and crossed back over to the hotel. When he reached the porch, he looked back to see Cox just closing his door. The lawman had waited until Clay had safely crossed the street.

He felt guilty about leaving Cox alone.

That was the trouble with Darringers. They never knew when to keep out of someone else's fight.

Inside the hotel, Clay went over to the desk, where the bespectacled man was half asleep in his chair. Clay awakened him, picked up his gear, and signed for a room overlooking the street.

He climbed the winding stairs to the landing and found his room. Settling in for the night, he found that the rope bed had a bumpy mattress, but he was too weary to care. He had forgotten to eat, but sleep overcame his hunger.

At first light on Sunday morning, dressed and washed, he went to the window to gaze into the street. The three young hands were coming from the doctor's office where Perkins was recovering.

The jail where Thatcher was locked up seemed quiet.

A few other men stirred in the streets. Two small children were running about, chased by a chubby woman. A wagon was rolling out of town, loaded with supplies.

Clay took his gear and left the room, walking down the stairs to the lobby. Several men and women were milling about. In the dining room's entrance, he saw Wes waving to him.

After depositing his gear at the desk and leaving his key with the sleepy clerk, Clay walked over to the lad.

"Miss Turner's inside," the youth told him.

"How is she?"

"Not so brave anymore. How we gonna protect her?"

"I don't know."

They walked into the dining room together. Several couples were seated at the tables. Katherine was near the back window, watching them approach. She was wearing her riding clothes. Her silken hair was drawn back from her pretty face. Her eyes were red from crying.

Clay sat down opposite her, and Wes sat at the side of the table, between them. The waiter brought the men coffee and refilled Katherine's cup. They ordered meat and eggs.

"How is Mr. Perkins?" she asked.

"I haven't seen him this morning. Last night, he was doin' fine."

"I'd like to see him before we go."

"No," Clay said. "We'll bring the horses to the hotel. You'll mount up and ride directly out of town."

"You're frightening me," she said.

"That's my intention," he told her.

"Clay's just trying to help," Wes added.

"I appreciate that," she responded. "But I can't just find a hole and hide."

"That's exactly what you're going to do," Clay said.

The bent waiter brought their breakfasts and more coffee. As they ate, Katherine kept glancing at Clay.

He felt uncomfortable under her scrutiny. Maybe she was expecting too much of him.

"Clay," Wes said, "I need a rifle."

"You stay with Miss Turner. I'll see what I can do."

After he downed his coffee and shoved his plate aside, Clay stood up, tipped his hat to Katherine, and left. He picked up his gear, including his Winchester, and walked out onto the porch. The sun was gathering the shadows and brightening the valley.

The three Turner hands were just down the street, waiting. One waved to him. Their horses were saddled.

He watched the townspeople moving about. Some were headed toward a little church up behind the houses on the west side of town. But for Katherine's problems, he would have been joining them.

Pausing to look northward, he saw two riders coming into town. One was a rough-looking young cowboy with his hat thrown back, devilment in his blue eyes.

The second rider was a pretty young woman, slim and tall, blond curls about her face and down her back, topped by a blue feathered hat. She had large blue eyes. Over her dress, she wore a long blue coat with velvet trim. She was riding sidesaddle and looked very much a lady.

Her mare was black with white stockings.

Looking directly at Clay, she smiled and reined up. The man with her also brought his mount up short, spinning about with curiosity.

"You must be Clay Darringer," she said.

Word had spread mighty fast. Clay didn't like that.

"I'm Susanna Renshaw. I've just returned from St. Louis. This is my brother Howie."

Clay tipped his hat, but he didn't speak.

"My father would like to talk with you," she said.

She suddenly stiffened, her glance passing him by. Clay turned to see Katherine in the doorway. The two women were looking each other over, and neither one was a bit friendly. Yet they smiled politely at each other.

"Mr. Darringer works for us," Katherine informed her.

Clay wanted to correct her, but at this point, he decided to keep his mouth shut.

"How unfortunate," Susanna replied. "And who are you?"

"Katherine Turner."

Susanna was startled, speechless as her mare danced about.

"Nice to see you, Miss Katherine," Howie said, straightening in the saddle as he tipped his hat. "I'll be calling soon's your brother allows."

Recovering, Susanna smiled briefly. "Nice to meet you, Miss Turner."

"Maybe you haven't heard," Katherine said coolly, "but my brother Sid was murdered on the trail."

"Sorry to hear that," Susanna said, frowning.

Abruptly, Susanna spun her horse about and rode south along the street, her brother reluctantly following.

Clay turned to look at Katherine. "Let's get this straight. I'm not working for you."

"I just wanted to let her know that I saw you first."

Clay was startled. She blushed at her words but stubbornly held her head high. He still wasn't used to her boldness.

Shaking his head, exasperated, he walked down the steps, leaving her to smile after him. He refused to look back.

He crossed over to the jail, finding the door open. Cox had just given the prisoner a tray of food. Thatcher was snarling even as he ate.

Clay and the lawman went back outside, out of earshot. There was no sign of Katherine at the moment.

"We'll be ridin' out shortly," Clay said. "Soon's I get the horses and see her foreman."

"Never mind Perkins. I'll keep an eye on him. You just get her out of town before anyone else learns she's here."

"The Renshaws know. We just met Susanna and her brother."

"Those men got a mean streak, but she's plenty sweet on her own. The only real lady we have around here. I mean, until Miss Turner came."

"You got a mighty strange valley here, Sheriff."

"Glad you like it." Cox grinned.

"Right now, I need a rifle for Wes."

Cox was agreeable, going back into the jail and returning with a Winchester.

"One of the early models," the lawman said, "but it'll do for the boy. It's loaded."

"Thanks. Now watch yourself."

"Likewise."

They shook hands, and Cox went back inside. Clay liked the lawman, and he worried about his longevity. Whoever had hired Thatcher would not be letting the big man go to trial.

Gear and rifles in hand, Clay headed down the boardwalk toward the livery. With the help of one of the Turner hands, he saddled the horses and loaded his gear. They led the animals into the busy street. Clay carried Wes's rifle.

At the hotel steps, the other two cowhands were waiting with their horses. All three had spent the night in the livery and looked a little rough.

Katherine was at the hotel entrance. At her side was Wes, who was carrying her carpetbag. Slowly, they came down the steps. Clay handed the old Winchester to the youth, who expressed his gratitude.

Clay was beginning to take a shine to Wes, but he wasn't planning to get involved with anyone at Castle Creek. He was moving on as soon as he was sure that Katherine was safe.

He told himself it was nothing more than gallantry.

Mounted, the six rode north. One of the hands rode point. Clay and Wes rode on either side of Katherine. The other hands brought up the rear.

The vast, rolling valley spread to the west and east. They rode along Castle Creek, which wound through the marshlike valley floor. The water in the creek was very low. Tracks of cattle that had come to the banks to drink were all around them. To the far north was the distant red and yellow rim.

Keyes, the young cowboy riding point, waved his hand eastward toward the lower eastern hills and prairie land. He reined his horse to be closer to the others.

"Most of that belongs to Wiley," he said. "He runs a lot of cattle out there, but if he had our water and grass, he'd triple his herd."

"What about the other ranchers?" Clay asked.

"Up ahead, through the valley and in the hills. Most of 'em run a good-size herd. Our closest neighbors are the Renshaws, north of us."

They soon turned left, riding westward toward the white-crested mountains. The rolling hills were still dry. Early blue and yellow flowers sprinkled the bushes and scattered plants. Junipers mingled with aspen, cottonwoods, and scrub oak.

"The best thing we got," Keyes said, "is White River. They call it that 'counta the rapids."

By late morning, they saw the distant hill where yellow aspen shimmered in the shape of a cross.

"Points right, toward the ranch," Keyes told them.

A long-eared rabbit leaped from the brush, startling Keyes's horse. In a wild, crazy pattern, the hare sped into the thickets. Overhead, a red-tailed hawk circled and then fluttered into a distant oak with a screech. The riders had interrupted its hunt.

At length, they rode into the area of the shimmering, golden aspens. Bluebirds with white bellies flittered in the higher limbs.

Riding over the hill, they could see cattle roaming the low, rolling land. Some were longhorns with big bones and sagging bellies. Others were whiteface Hereford stock. Most were a crazy mixture. Clay guessed he was looking at a couple of hundred head.

"All together," Keyes said, "we got about four thousand head, maybe a little more, scattered all over. We get most of 'em at roundup, though, when we hire on a lot more hands."

"You get a lot of snow?" Clay asked.

"Higher up, mostly. A pond we got out there ices up. But the snow melts off down here."

They skirted the herd and moved over the next rise. Here they reined up to view the ranch. The house and sheds were indeed circled by a high wall. It looked like an old fort. Outside the walls were corrals, a barn, the bunkhouse, and other outbuildings. Everything was spread over one large, rolling hill.

Two riders had come out to greet them. These men were older and more seasoned. At the barn, they all dismounted, leaving their horses to Keyes. Carrying their gear, Clay and Wes walked with Katherine toward the ranch walls, which appeared to be nearly twelve feet high.

One of the oldtimers went with them, carrying a rifle and opening the heavy, wagon-size gate in the eastern wall. Once they were inside, he shoved the gate closed.

The courtyard could have been in Mexico. Flowers and cactus were thick along the inside walls. Three maple trees, their leaves scarlet, graced a picnic area in the center.

Next to a water pump and well was a dry fish pond, circled by colorful rocks. Near it was a forgotten fountain graced by a statue of a Grecian lady. The yard was maybe two hundred feet wide north to south and twice that east to west.

"They used to have dances here," the old cowhand said.

There were narrow platforms just high enough for a man to see over the walls. A guard was posted near the gate, resting his elbow on the top crossboard.

Set twenty feet from the western wall and shaded by a cottonwood on each side, the two-story ranch house was at least a hundred feet wide, clearing the north and south walls by fifty feet. It rose above the twelve-foot fortress walls.

Their escort walked onto the porch and banged on the door. An armed man opened it. Introductions were made, and the two hands stayed outside as Katherine, Wes, and Clay entered. Clay and Wes set their gear just inside.

The huge front room was nicely furnished with stuffed chairs and a couch. A great horn chair sat by the open hearth, where logs burned slowly. Hides carpeted the hard wooden floor. A stairway was in the far right corner.

Seated asleep in the horn chair was Katherine's brother Jacob. In his early thirties, he looked pale and gaunt, fully dressed but wrapped in blankets. Hesitantly Katherine moved forward and knelt at his side.

"Jacob?"

Her brother jerked slightly, then looked at her. He had hazel, questioning eyes. His face would be handsome when he regained his strength. His nose was slightly crooked, his jaw square. Receding red-brown hair lay back from a wrinkled brow.

"Katherine?"

She took his hand in hers, and he brightened. Then he grinned, touching her face with his free hand.

"Doggoned if you ain't beautiful," he said.

"Jacob, are you all right?"

He nodded and bent forward, drawing her into his arms. She sobbed out the story of Sid's death and how she had shot Sheb Wiley. She added that they had seen Wiley at Camp Grant, causing Sid to turn toward Bravo Canyon. She also told him she had seen Tuck Wiley and the Renshaws.

He held her tight, their faces together as they both wept. They clung together in the painful knowledge that they were the only survivors of their family.

Clay looked away, hurting. Wes was pale.

Finally Katherine drew back and gestured to her new friends. Tears were still trickling down her face. Jacob had no color. Wes came forward to shake Jacob's hand.

"This is Wes Barnes," Katherine said. "He lost his family when the Apache came through where his father had a mine. He was the only survivor."

"Welcome, Wes," Jacob greeted. "Why don't you move in with us? We got plenty of room. And plenty of work."

Wes fought his tears, nodding his gratitude.

"They caught a man in town last night after he shot Mr. Perkins in the foot," she said. "A man named Thatcher, who claimed he'd been fired by the Wileys and only had a few days of work left. It'll be a while before Mr. Perkins will be back here."

"Blast."

"And Jacob," she added, "this is Clay Darringer."

Her brother brightened. "I'm glad you're here, Darringer."

"No, Jacob," she said. "It's not what you think. After we were attacked in the canyon, I was the only survivor, because they thought I was dead. I was out of my head from being hit so hard and from the heat. I took up an old pistol and started after the killers."

"Katherine!" Jacob said with concern.

"I didn't know," she continued, "that there were Apaches at the head of the canyon. I would have walked right into them. Mr. Darringer was up on the cliff and safe, but he came down and picked me up. He saved my life, Jacob."

Jacob extended his hand. Clay came forward to shake it.

"Thank you," Jacob said earnestly.

"He's only here," she added, "until you're well."

"He's on his way to California," Wes contributed.

They all looked at Clay, who felt mighty uncomfortable.

"Thank you," Jacob said. "You can stay here with us."

"Clay studied medicine," Katherine informed her brother. "Maybe he should look at your injuries."

Jacob was surprised but shook his head. "Doc said I just have to get my strength back. I lost a lot of blood. But now that you're here, Katherine, I'll get well mighty fast. Especially if they taught you to cook at that finishing school."

Katherine shook her head. "No, they only taught us how to pour tea. But I cooked at home."

"Well, I ain't had breakfast," Jacob said. "Cook room's right over there to the left."

"As soon as I freshen up," she said, smiling.

"Go ahead, you and Wes pick your rooms out. I want to talk to Clay."

Wes took Clay's gear, and Katherine picked up her heavy carpetbag. Together, they went up the stairs.

When they were out of sight, Jacob turned to Clay, who had knelt to stoke up the fire in the hearth.

"Your reputation could help us, Clay."

"I'm not for hire."

"But just having you here might force these killers to sit back and think awhile. They've hit us pretty hard. And I heard somebody sent for some fast gun. Don't know which one."

"Well, Carmody's in town. He rode part way with us."

"He's a bad one," Jacob said, frowning.

"Your biggest worry right now is your sister."

"I know they'll be takin' another crack at me, but you're sayin' they'll come after her as well?"

"Yes."

Jacob studied him. "And that's why you stayed?"

Clay nodded, and rose slowly from the hearth. He sat down in a chair opposite Jacob.

Jacob shoved his blankets away from his wide chest as the fire grew hotter. His face was tight with lines as he spoke.

"You think Carmody would go after my sister?"

"Not with a gun. Tell me about the Wileys."

"Ole Tate Wiley has three boys. One's off in military school. The other two boys are just like Tate, plenty tough, and all three are fancy with a gun. They moved in about four years ago, bought out the former owner, and started filing on every inch of land they could get. Ole Tate can't build his herd any bigger where he is. He wants this spread."

"And your river."

"Prettiest thing you ever saw," Jacob said.

"How do you keep the other herds from just moving in?"

"Been doin' it with a big bluff and a good sheriff. But what we got now is barbed wire. We strung one fence between us and Renshaw's on the north. Made 'em plenty mad. We got lots more to string."

Clay didn't answer. He hated barbed wire.

"Anybody with cattle in this valley could be trying to kill us off," Jacob said. "They figure they wipe out the Turners, this place could go at auction. But there'll be a big fight first, everyone tryin' to move in and take possession."

"The Wileys would be the strongest?"

"Them or the Renshaws."

"We met Miss Renshaw and her brother in town."

"Mighty pretty, ain't she?"

"You've been noticin', have you?"

"Who hasn't? But she don't take much shine to me."

"Maybe you're lucky," Clay said, grinning.

"But ole Howie, he took a shine to my sister, figurin' if he married her, he'd get a foothold here. He ain't so bad, I reckon, but I told him he'd have to mend his ways before he comes around here. He's always into gamblin' and fightin'."

"I hear the Wileys were after her as well."

"Sheb come over first. I didn't trust him, and told him so. Tuck was kind of fun, but I finally run him off as well. I told ole Tuck he didn't have the brains of a tomcat. Made 'im pretty mad."

Abruptly, the men stopped talking. Katherine was coming down the stairs, with Wes following.

More cheerful now, she smiled and came to kiss Jacob's cheek. "Breakfast coming up," she said.

Wes went out to help her. The door closed behind them as they entered the room to the far left.

Jacob turned to consider Clay as he spoke.

"What's this about you having studied medicine?"

"Tried it a year, but felt rotten when people died. And when they couldn't save my wife and unborn child, I gave it up. Bein' a doctor takes more guts than I have."

"I doubt that," Jacob said. "I suspect you have a need for perfection. But it's not a perfect world, Clay."

"Reckon not."

"So what are your plans?"

"Got in mind to buy some land out California way, or maybe up in Oregon. I scouted for the Army a long time. Saved 'most everything I earned."

"You don't sound much like a gunfighter. Are you fast?"

"Fast enough."

"Faster than Carmody?"

"I don't know, but there's a lot more to a gunfight than speed."

"You figure the sheriff can keep Thatcher in jail?"

"No, I don't. The circuit judge comes on Friday. I figure to ride into town tonight."

About that time, Wes came out with two trays of steaming bacon and eggs. Clay was delighted.

Wes went back to the kitchen while the men devoured the delicious food. Between bites, Jacob told Clay that he was certain the farmers were not in on the killing. They were religious people who kept to themselves.

Later, their stomachs full, Jacob and Clay enjoyed the hot coffee that Katherine served, her little finger crooked as she tried to steady the heavy pot.

"They taught us how to do this," she said cheerfully.

"Say now," Jacob queried, "you sent word you wanted to come here after our aunt died, but you never told us why you left that finishin' school."

She glanced at Clay's slow smile. Bravely, she answered. "Jacob, your sister was asked to leave. Seems nice ladies stay behind their fans and don't speak up. And when the schoolmistress's husband tries to grab you in the hallway, you're not supposed to knock him down."

Jacob laughed. "You're a Turner, all right. Half Irish and half everything else, but all ornery."

She smiled as Wes dragged a chair forward so that she could sit with them. Clay was seeing her more in depth. Yes, she was direct and forward and unafraid, but she was more woman than he had realized.

"So you really knocked him down?" Wes persisted.

Katherine nodded, then laughed. "I shoved him back, then hit him with my fist, right on the jaw, while he was off balance. Almost broke my hand. He just kept on falling. He was the most surprised man you ever saw."

Everyone laughed, and she told more stories about the school. Then they talked about the river and pond.

"I'd like to take a look," Clay said.

"By golly, I'm goin' with you," Jacob decided, shoving his blankets aside. "I'm sick and tired of sittin' here."

"Tomorrow," Katherine said.

Jacob grimaced, then nodded. "You're right."

"And I'm going with you," she added.

"You are not," Jacob said firmly.

Katherine merely smiled and poured him more coffee.

"I'd like to rest my roan," Clay told him. "But if you have a horse I could borrow, I'll ride back into town and see if the sheriff needs help. Looks like you have enough men here, at least for tonight."

"Take a couple of men with you," Jacob said.

"I'll go," Wes offered.

But Clay would have none of it, and insisted on going alone. He didn't want to take any men from their guard.

He was given a big bay gelding. Taking his Winchester, he mounted and sat tall in the saddle in front of the house, looking down at Katherine, Wes, and her brother.

"I may stay at the jail tonight," he said.

Katherine was in such distress that he made a hurried departure. He set the bay into a lope, riding out of the enclosure and a long way down the hill before he dared look back.

She was standing alone in front of the gate, arms folded, watching him fade out of sight. It pained him to know she was there.

But now he wondered if she had sensed some terrible danger.

Chapter Five

*S*unday evening in Castle Creek was quiet as a graveyard. Clay rode slowly into town at twilight. He had taken a few hours to scout the hills and get the lay of the land.

Now the hair was tight on the back of his neck. The bay gelding took deliberate steps, as if sensing danger. Entering town from the north, Clay came almost at once to the sheriff's office on the right. Lamps burned low behind the shuttered windows.

Across the street, the hotel was brightly lit. Stores and other buildings on either side were dark except for the occasional street lamps, but further down, the saloons were aglow.

Clay reined up in front of the jail and dismounted. The only other horses and wagons were farther down the street. It was almost as if the area was being avoided.

He tied the reins loosely to the hitching rail and walked quietly onto the boardwalk. He paused when a sweet female voice called to him.

"Mr. Darringer."

Awkwardly, he turned to look across the street.

84

Standing on the hotel steps was Susanna Renshaw, hatless and framed by the lights.

Ill at ease, he crossed the street to the foot of the steps and stopped, still standing in the dirt. She moved so that a nearby lamp cast light on her pretty face.

"I would like to speak with you," she said.

"Be safer for you inside the hotel."

"Are you dangerous?"

"I wasn't thinkin' of me," he said. "There's going to be trouble."

"Because of that man in jail?"

Clay nodded, looking down the silent, empty street.

"Have you been reading dime novels?" she asked, still smiling. She came down two steps; there was only one to go.

Clay was nervous at her nearness, but didn't move.

"I have to go now, ma'am."

"Susanna. And you're on the wrong side, Mr. Darringer."

"I'm not sure of that."

She moved to the bottom step, starlight in her golden hair. Clay wanted to back up, but he was transfixed by her sweet scent and the sudden touch of her hand on his arm.

"I wish you'd work for us," she said.

Clay swallowed hard. With great courage, he escaped her touch, tipped his hat, and turned to cross the street. He didn't look back until he was at the sheriff's door. She was gone.

He drew a breath of relief and knocked.

A shuttered window slid back just enough for light to fall on Clay's face. Then the window closed and the door opened. Clay entered, finding Sheriff Cox alone in the room.

In the back cell, snoring softly, was Thatcher.

Cox shook his hand, then returned to sit behind his desk. Clay sat down in one of the chairs facing him.

"How's Perkins?" Clay asked.

"Rantin' and ravin'. He wants to get back to the ranch. He's worried about Miss Turner. Whoever's behind this ain't gonna want her or Thatcher to do any talkin', that's for sure. But first, they gotta get Thatcher."

"It'll be tonight," Clay said. "The street's been cleared this end of town."

"I had that feelin'. You gonna stick around?"

"I don't figure I got any choice."

Cox leaned back in his squeaky chair, studying Clay as he spoke. "I know. I had your measure when I first saw you. With Miss Turner, it's Texas gallantry. But when it comes to Thatcher, you're honor bound to fight. Your reputation doesn't do you justice."

Clay was embarrassed at the direct praise. He shifted his weight in his chair and looked around the room. It was close enough to a fortress.

"I thought I was gonna round up a couple of deputies," the lawman said. "Couldn't get one volunteer. Didn't want any man I had to railroad into this."

"I'll stay the night, soon's I take care of my horse,"

Clay told him. "I figure whoever hired Thatcher, they'll be wantin' to sneak in after dark."

"They gotta get through that door," Cox said.

The sudden deafening explosion blew the door and front wall right at them, knocking them to the floor with a thunderous roar. The world vibrated. Boards, dust, and debris covered them like an avalanche. Clay lost his hearing for just a moment. He was shaking all over.

The sheriff was crumpled against the wall behind the desk, unconscious and bleeding.

Dazed, Clay was struggling up from under the door when he saw the three men entering, their faces covered with bandannas.

They started firing. Clay raised the shattered door for protection, drawing and firing back, but he was too dazed to aim straight. Some of their shots slammed into the jail cell and the startled Thatcher, who crashed backwards in the cell.

Clay got one of the men in the shoulder as they ran back outside. He thrust the door aside, breathing hard as he staggered toward the open wall. He stumbled onto the boardwalk, leaning on the hitching rail to steady himself.

His horse, having been set free before the blast, came nervously up to the railing.

The three outlaws were riding out of town, disappearing into the darkness. Clay fired at their dust, then hesitated. He was still dazed and didn't know the terrain. Even if he were able to follow, he could be set up for ambush.

Still shaken, he was aware of men running from the hotel.

He turned, reentering the shattered office. As he stepped over the broken wall, holstering his gun, he saw Thatcher sprawled in the cell.

Clay kneeled behind the desk and found that a window frame had struck Sheriff Cox in the neck. He was bleeding profusely. Pressing his finger on the artery, Clay managed to stop the flow of blood.

Four townsmen came crawling over the debris.

"Get the doc," Clay told them urgently.

"Dynamite," a fat merchant said. "That's what they used. And Thatcher's shot dead."

Still kneeling with the lawman, Clay realized his right shoulder hurt from being struck by the door. This was the wrong time for his gun hand to be slowed.

By the time Doc Miller came, Clay's head was clear.

"You saved his life," the old doctor said, kneeling at Cox's side. "He'll be all right, but we'd better get him to my office now that the bleeding's stopped."

Clay stood up as the townsmen carried the unconscious lawman outside.

He and the doctor opened the cell to look at Thatcher, who was still. They were alone in the building as the doctor turned the big man over on the bunk.

"Shot twice in the shoulder and once in the arm," the doctor said. "But he's sure enough alive."

"We've got to keep it quiet," Clay told him.

"Who can we trust?"

"No one."

"Well, he oughta be able to walk, once he comes to," Doc Miller said as he tended Thatcher with alcohol and tight bandages. "You get him over to my office in about an hour. I'll make sure no one's there."

"Circuit judge comes on Friday. You think he'll be able to stand trial?" Clay asked.

"Most likely."

"You go ahead, Doctor. I'll keep an eye out here. If those men ask about Thatcher, tell them you want the body for some tests and to leave him alone. Maybe tomorrow, you can bury a closed casket."

The doctor nodded. He gave Clay some smelling salts, and then turned out the lamps as he left.

The room remained totally dark. The only light came from the hotel, its glow soft on the collapsed wall. A few curious men came to stand on the boardwalk. They couldn't see Clay in the cell.

Soon the street was silent, empty.

Thatcher was still unconscious. Clay turned the big man on his side and put handcuffs on both wrists behind his back. Then he propped him up against the wall. He opened the smelling salts, holding them to Thatcher's nose.

Coughing, almost heaving, the big man tossed his head. He tried to rise, then gasped in pain.

"Take it easy," Clay said. "Your friends just tried to deal you out."

Truth hit Thatcher hard. "You gotta get me outa here."

"We're going to the doc's. Can you walk?"

Clay helped him to his feet. They left the jail cell

and climbed over the debris, venturing carefully onto the boardwalk. The moon had disappeared behind drifting clouds.

Except for the lamps here and there along the street, it was dark. There was no one in sight. Thatcher was in a lot of pain, staggering crazily as Clay pushed him to greater speed.

They were soon at the stairs to the doctor's office. Clay had to use all his strength to push the big man up the steps, one at a time. Thatcher's weight often fell back on Clay's hands and his sore right shoulder.

Finally, they reached the landing. But just then they heard voices coming from a saloon across the street, the one where Thatcher had been caught. Clay shoved the big man against the wall, into the darkness.

Two men came out, mounted their horses, and rode north.

When the street was silent again, Clay moved his prisoner on to the doctor's office door, shoving it open. There was no light in the room as he pushed Thatcher inside and closed the door. Then the lamp was turned up by the doctor.

Perkins was sitting in a chair, his bandaged leg on a footstool. Sheriff Cox was lying on a long table. The townspeople had left. Clay pushed his prisoner over to a chair, forcing him to sit.

"Who done it?" the foreman demanded.

"They had their faces covered," Clay said, "but there were three of 'em."

The awakening lawman was listening, trying to sit

up. The doctor ordered him to stay prone, then told him that Clay had saved his life.

"They get away?" Cox asked, blinking.

Clay nodded. The doctor turned his attention to Thatcher, removing the bandages, poking around for the bullets.

"Hey, that hurts," Thatcher growled.

"You were almost in a condition where you wouldn't feel anything," the doctor told him. "Be glad you're alive."

"Why, so you can hang me?" the prisoner snapped.

"Attempted murder don't necessarily mean hangin'," Cox pointed out, rising on his elbow.

"I ain't shot nobody," Thatcher said.

"You ready to tell me who hired you?" Cox asked.

"I don't know nothin'. But you gotta get me outa town. I'll stand trial, but somewhere else."

"We wouldn't get you half a mile," Cox said. "Your best bet is to stay right here."

Thatcher yelped as the doctor seized a bullet and pulled it free. Finished, Miller bandaged the big man once more.

"Don't be movin' around much," the doctor cautioned. "You might start bleeding again."

Clay took the prisoner into a windowless room where there was an iron bedstead. He cuffed the man to the post between railings, where the irons would not come free.

"Don't worry," Clay said. "They'll bury an empty casket tomorrow."

Thatcher, relieved and exhausted, stretched out

and closed his eyes. He had committed a crime, but he deserved a fair trial.

After closing the door on the prisoner, Clay turned to Cox. "You plan to stay here?"

"At least tonight," Cox said. "I know a couple of men I can trust. The mercantile has a storeroom we can use. Tomorrow night, we'll transfer him."

"Just be careful," Clay told him. "Now I'd better get back to the ranch."

"Any sign of Carmody in town?" the lawman asked.

"No," Clay said. "And this attack wasn't his style."

"Let's get my horse," Perkins said. "I'm goin' back with you tonight. Whoever's doin' this is gettin' mighty bold."

The doctor made a fuss, but Perkins was adamant.

Clay and the foreman left the group and went back down the stairs and over to the jail. Clay put Perkins on his bay and led the horse down to the livery, where he saddled the man's sorrel. Clay mounted Perkins's horse.

"I got me a gut feeling," Perkins told him. "Let's ride."

Clay didn't mention that he had the same sense of unease, for the hair on the back of his neck was tightening, a sure sign of trouble.

He was glad when they finally reached the grove of aspens that pointed to the ranch. It was moonlight, the sky sprinkled with stars, often covered by moving clouds. There was a chill in the air.

"Storm's comin'," Perkins noted. "Maybe if they get their creeks filled up, we'll have a winter's rest."

"They got a campaign goin'," Clay said. "I don't figure they'll be stoppin' what they set out to do. They've gone too far."

"Now you mention it, old Tate Wiley was an Army officer."

They rode through the aspens. It was then that they saw a red and white glow in the hills ahead.

"Dag nab it," Perkins snarled.

Now they could hear gunfire. They set their horses to a lope, covering the hills as fast as they could. On the rise just before the ranch, they slowed. Now they were over the crest.

About a dozen men on horseback were circling the Turners' walls, firing sporadically. Gunfire was being returned from inside. The bunkhouse was burning. Smoke rose from the bright flames. The light sprinkled on the riders, giving the scene an eerie look.

One of the raiders was lighting another torch. As the man headed for the walls, Clay leaned over to the bay and pulled his Winchester from the scabbard.

"They're out of range," Perkins said.

Clay aimed high, slowly lowered the sights, drew a deep breath, and fired.

The man was thrown sideways from the saddle; he crashed to the ground, taking the torch with him. Another rider sped to his side and bent down to grab the torch. Clay fired again. The second man fell from the saddle.

Other riders returned to scoop up the two

wounded, taking their horses in tow. Clay fired again. The riders took off at a gallop, heading north.

"I'd like to foller 'em right back to Wiley's ranch," Perkins snarled.

"Don't matter who sent 'em. You'd just be riding into an ambush," Clay said.

They set their mounts at a lope and were soon within shouting distance. Men had come from behind the walls to rush over to the burning bunkhouse. It was chaos.

Perkins headed for the firefighters, and Clay headed for the now open gate. He reined up and dismounted, still carrying the repeating rifle as he hurried into the enclosure.

Keyes came running to meet him. "We was all havin' supper inside with the Turners," he said. "Lucky for us."

"Any get in here?"

"No."

"Recognize any of 'em?"

"They all had their faces covered."

Clay asked Keyes to stay near the gate, which they closed. Then he headed for the house.

Jacob was there, rifle in hand, his face dark with fury. But he was glad to see Clay.

"They're gone," Clay said.

Katherine and Wes were coming down the stairs. Each was carrying a rifle. Clay felt awkward, as if his concern for her had been foolish. At the same time, he was glad to see her unharmed.

They gathered around the hearth, Katherine's gaze

fixed on him. He tried not to look at her as he told them about Cox and Thatcher.

"Dirty buzzards," Jacob muttered. "That does it. We need our own army."

Wes went into the kitchen to heat up some of the leftover supper, and Katherine went to get the medicine chest. Clay sat down opposite Jacob and rubbed his sore right shoulder.

"They'll just pick you off one at a time," Clay said.

"So what you figure we oughta do?" Jacob asked.

"We have to get to the source."

"How we gonna do that?" Jacob persisted.

"I don't know the country," Clay said. "Tomorrow, I'll do some ridin'."

He wasn't prepared for Katherine's being upset about his sore shoulder. Despite his protest, she insisted on his removing his shirt.

Embarrassed by his broad hairy chest and muscled arms, he sat transfixed while she rubbed alcohol on his right shoulder and applied hot towels. All the while, he refused to look at her. Her fingers were firm, digging into his flesh. Clay found himself holding his breath every few minutes.

"You did the same for me, remember?" she asked.

Clay was glad when Jacob didn't pursue that remark. Instead, her brother was amused, enjoying the show. When finally she tried to put Clay's shirt back on, Clay refused her help and would not look at her.

After Clay had something to eat, Katherine sat near him on a stool, talking about the river and pond. He insisted that she and Jacob should stay on the ranch where it was safe.

"But I can fire a rifle," she insisted. "Jacob taught me."

"You're a target," Clay said firmly. "You are not going."

And so it was that on Monday morning, right after sunup, Clay, Katherine, Wes, and Keyes rode into the hills, heading west. Clay was on his blue roan, Katherine on the sorrel mare with a food basket. Keyes and Wes were riding bays. Each carried a slicker, as it had rained during the night.

Jacob had remained in bed, sound asleep, the fight having exhausted him.

Keyes took them southwest through the rolling hills, reining up on the edge of an arroyo to look down at White River on its journey from the distant mountains. Roaring with foaming rapids, it ranged from ten feet wide in the canyon to triple that as it spread out and slowed down through its own wide, pretty valley dotted with cattle, moving like crystal toward the wide horizon.

"All that land is ours," Katherine told Clay, waving her hand south and westward. "As far as you can see."

"That river's the best thing we got," Keyes said. "Our cattle always got water. But when it gets way out yonder on the prairie, it starts to disappear as it goes along."

"There's a really pretty view up there," Katherine added, pointing to the rugged terrain higher up in the north. There were more boulders and heavy brush than trees.

Keyes turned his horse about, bringing them back

to the trail. They climbed for an hour, at times nearly straight up, the terrain rugged with brush, rocks, and juniper. It was cold and damp, the dark sky threatening.

Before turning into the wooded area, they paused to look at the valley in all directions. From the northern rim to the prairie, it was beautiful, but there was nothing prettier than the white rapids and clear water of the river running south through Turner land.

They rode on level ground at last, a wide, rolling sea of grass with cattle grazing to their left.

Clay reined up, staring at the dark blue pond. It was a little over one hundred feet in circumference, in a great hollow surrounded by rocky but rolling, grassy, and wooded terrain. In the west, forested snowcaps towered in the background.

"It's fed by springs," Keyes said. "All the fellas like to ride herd up here in the summer. They sneak a swim every chance they get. 'Course now it's gettin' too cold."

They rode down to the pond, circling it.

Once they were on the northern hillside, they dismounted. Loosening the cinch on each horse, they walked to the edge of the pond. The dark sky made the water a deep blue-black. It was beautiful.

Clay knelt to study prints in the soft dirt and dry mud.

"Bear," he said. "Cougar. Mule deer."

He stood and moved along the bank, then knelt again.

"Men and horses. Chipmunks. And a gray fox."

Katherine was fascinated. "How can you tell?"

"Well," he said, "each animal has its own sign. Take a look at that bear track. She kind of ambles along. She's plenty big. Five-toed tracks. Hind paws look almost human. If it's a female, there'll be a couple of tiny cubs around February. She's probably fattening up on nuts and berries."

"What about the other prints?"

"Well, you take those tracks over there. Mule deer, most likely. They put their feet down different than whitetail when runnin'. That's a cougar track there, slow and cautious, but its prints have been pretty blown over, while the deer's is fresh. See how it kicked some little rocks out of their sockets?"

He explained the others, then realized he was almost boasting about his knowledge. He was showing off for her.

Embarrassed, he stood to gaze at the surrounding hills. Cattle grazed in the wooded heights. He could envision a house on that highest hill in a circle of aspens. Startled by the thought, he refused to look at Katherine until she spoke.

"Isn't it beautiful?" she asked.

He turned to see the wind blowing her red hair back from her freckled face. Even in her riding outfit, she was more lovely than a man could handle.

Abruptly, the drizzle started.

"Any good place to sit it out?" Clay asked.

"Way back, there's a hollow in a canyon wall," Keyes replied.

They tightened the cinches and mounted. As they rode up through the trees, they pulled on their slickers. Katherine had difficulty and was soaked by the time she had hers in place. The wind was blowing hard now. The rain was heavy. Lightning flashed in the distant sky.

They hurried through the woods to a great wall of stone. A huge, high-ceilinged hollow in the granite was nearly a cave, going back fifteen feet on a downward slope. It was at least thirty feet wide, so they brought their horses in with them and dismounted. The rain was suddenly lighter, slowing to a sprinkle outside their haven.

The horses were kept to one side and hobbled. Because Katherine had been soaked, Clay made a fire of some old brush that had been blown into the cavern. They had their picnic, Katherine entertaining Keyes with stories of life in Kansas. By the time they had finished, the rain had slowed to a sprinkle.

Suddenly the blue roan began to hop about, snorting, tossing his head. The other horses were frightened, dancing around, fighting their hobbles. The men sprang to their feet. Keyes ran to calm the frantic horses.

"Bear," Clay said, wondering if he had time to get the Winchester out of his saddle. He drew his Colt.

"Wait," Wes urged, turning to the campfire.

The sudden specter of the giant black sow was terrifying. On its hind legs, it stood nearly seven feet high. It waddled forth with a horrible roar, blocking the outside light. Nothing was going to stop its furious charge.

Clay sprang in front of Katherine and Wes.

Ignoring the horses, the bear came straight at Clay. He aimed his Colt, knowing he'd have to empty it into the charging beast, but it wouldn't be enough to stop her. She was but a few feet away as Clay started to fire.

But Wes darted around Clay with a great bundle of burning brush, which he thrust at the bear. With a piglike squeal, the beast clawed at the fire that had landed on her chest. She staggered backward into the light rain, her furry body aflame as she clawed away the brush.

As the rain wet the smoking fire, Clay was able to grab his rifle from Keyes's hands and aim at the bear's head. The beast suddenly dropped to all fours with an anguished snort. Before Clay could get a good shot, the animal roared, reared up, still clawing at her smoking chest, and turned away, dropping again to her four legs and lumbering off into the rain.

Clay slowly lowered his weapon, watching the bear go out of sight. Then he turned. Wes was sitting on his heels and wrapping his arms about himself in pain. The boy had picked up the burning brush with his bare hands. Katherine, badly shaken, was hugging his shoulders.

Clay pulled Wes out into the rain, holding up his hands to the cold drops.

"Keep them wet," Clay said. "When you get back to the ranch, use lime water and linseed oil. Maybe Katherine can make a paste of cookin' soda."

"That was a brave thing you did," Katherine told Wes.

"Maybe," the youth said, "but it was Clay jumped in front of us."

"And I thank you, again," Katherine said to Clay.

Clay looked out at the drizzling rain. The storm appeared to be breaking up. It was almost noon. He could do a lot of riding before dark.

"All three of you," Clay ordered, "head back to the ranch."

He refused all argument. Wes's hands needed treatment. Keyes was required to protect Katherine. The bear could return.

After Keyes gave him directions to Renshaw's, Clay went to his roan. "Don't wait for the rain to stop," he told the group. "No tellin' when that bear will be back."

"But why would it come back?" Katherine asked nervously.

"Because we invaded her den."

"We sure did," Wes said.

Before Clay could mount, Katherine was at his side. Her green eyes were glistening. She looked worried. Her concern made him feel awkward, embarrassed, a little cornered.

"I'll be back tonight," he said.

"Please be careful," Katherine pleaded.

"I'm just gettin' the lay of the land."

Keyes came forward. "I wouldn't go past the wire if I was you. The Renshaws are plenty hot since we put it up. And Howie's pretty fancy with his six-gun."

Clay shrugged. He had heard so much talk about valley men with fast guns that he was beginning to discount it. Carmody would be the one to watch.

When all were mounted, Clay said farewell, and rode north without looking back.

The rain had stopped. Dark clouds had turned to white and given way to the sun. He rode down through the hills, enjoying the sight of cattle grazing. There was good grass here. At least the Turners had not overstocked their range.

Water was still running down the gullies and creeks.

By late afternoon, Clay was in sight of the barbed wire, which ran downhill from west to east. Some of it was attached to trees, the rest to posts set solidly in the rocky ground. At some points, there were rock fences to supplement the four strands of vicious wire.

Clay hated barbed wire, but he understood Turner's reasoning. Still, if the rancher had seen men wrapped in the brutal barbs during a range war, he might have been more reluctant to string it.

Clay was not surprised to find, deep in a hollow, that the wire had been cut wide enough for a dozen head of cattle to pass at a time.

The rain had washed away most of the signs, but Clay could see that a herd had recently passed through onto Turner land, and retreated after a good graze.

He rode through the opening onto Renshaw land. It was pretty much downhill all the way. That old warning sign, the tightening of hair on the back of his neck, was again telling him to turn back.

He had ridden barely an hour when he first saw the Renshaw herd, grazing up in the wooded hillsides. He reined up to rest his roan, enjoying the sight of the cattle.

A sudden harsh voice broke the stillness.

"Reach, mister!"

Chapter Six

*T*urning in the saddle, Clay looked at the man with the rifle. It was Howie Renshaw, sitting a sorrel and looking mighty unfriendly as he rode out of a gully.

Clay sat calm, his hands on the pommel. He had never in his life lifted his hands under threat. He wasn't starting now. That irritated Howie, who grudgingly lowered his rifle.

"What you want here, Darringer?"

"Just seein' the valley."

"Well, you ain't welcome, 'less you're changin' sides."

Howie's face was rough, barely shaven and slightly crooked. He had blue eyes like his sister, but his were narrowed and crowded by crinkled skin.

"I figured on meetin' your father," Clay said.

"Well, maybe he'll talk sense to yuh. Come on."

They rode side by side through the wet grass and scattered trees. At times they were high and clear of the terrain, enough to see the sprawling valley.

"Our place goes past Castle Rocks," Howie said. "Then you run into Crumley's, then Lycomb's, and Pensetter's and Coghram's. Across the valley, there are some other ranchers afore you get to Wiley's, but the Wiley bunch, they got half the valley over there."

"You have a nice ranch here. Don't see why you need Turner land."

"For your information, I figure on marryin' into that spread."

"You figure she'll have you?"

"Why not? I'm a mighty handsome feller."

Clay was finding it hard to dislike the homely man, but he reserved judgment. They rode over more hills as the sun began to cast long shadows. It was twilight when they came in sight of the ranch.

The buildings and corrals were set on knolls to avoid flash floods. The old house was large, rambling, as if it had been added to over the years. Cattle roamed the hills nearby.

Alone in one of the corrals as they approached, a seasoned black stallion tossed his head and trotted about. He had a star on his face and white stockings. A beautiful animal, he had to be fifteen years old.

"Renshaw's Pride," Howie said.

Clay could see other blacks, one with white stockings, mingling in the other corrals with sorrels and bays. The muddy ground was spotted with puddles of water.

Men came out of the bunkhouse to watch them ride in. On the front porch of the big house, a cowhand was soaping a saddle, but stopped as they approached. At Howie's signal, he left his chore and went over to join the other hands.

Clay dismounted and threw a stirrup over the

horn, pausing to loosen the cinch. His roan bit at him, then tossed its head.

The door opened, and Susanna appeared in blue gingham, her blond hair up in pretty curls. She smiled at Clay as he and Howie came up the steps.

"How nice of you to stop by," she said to Clay.

Howie followed as she led Clay into the big front room of the house. A fire was crackling in the stone hearth. A small Mexican woman stopped her dusting and disappeared.

Coming from a back room was Hack Renshaw, a sixtyish man old beyond his years. He was gray, wrinkled, and stooped, and not very friendly as Susanna introduced the visitor.

They sat in chairs near the hearth. Hack looked Clay over solemnly as Susanna tried to make their guest feel at home. The Mexican woman served him coffee. The others just glared.

"So," Hack growled, "I hear someone's hired Carmody, and now Turner's got you."

"I'm not on hire," Clay told him. "I'm just here until Miss Turner and Jacob are safe."

"Yeah, I heard they lost Sid," Hack said, "right after someone nearly got Jacob. And I hear Thatcher took a potshot at Perkins, then got shot down hisself in a jailbreak."

"Someone used dynamite," Clay said. "Was that you?"

Hack stiffened in his chair, blue eyes darkening.

"Listen to me, Darringer," he growled. "When I wanta kill a man, I do it face on, and don't you forget it."

"And your son?" Clay asked.

Both Renshaw men sat stiff and glaring. It was Susanna's soft voice that calmed things.

"Mr. Darringer, you're our guest. Please don't offend our hospitality. You'll stay for supper, of course."

Clay glanced at her. She was sure pretty, and feminine, and a lady. He found himself making comparisons to Katherine's boldness. He was a little more comfortable with Susanna.

Despite the unfriendly men in the house, Clay stayed for supper, prepared by the Mexican woman. Hack constantly talked about the White River and how Turner was hogging the best land. He also was angry about the fence.

"Barbed wire," Hack growled. "Ain't nothin' meaner."

"We tried to buy out ole man Turner," Howie said. "So did the Wileys. He wouldn't have none of it. Just sittin' up there with all that water and grass. Won't even sell us a license to graze up there."

"You've water in the creeks now," Clay pointed out.

"Sure, but I still gotta keep my herd down to size," Hack grunted. "I had big ideas when I came here and enough money to build up, but all I got's a few creeks and some waterholes this time o' year."

"I don't reckon that's Turner's fault," Clay said.

"Is that all you men can talk about?" Susanna asked. "Mr. Darringer has been traveling. He must have things to tell us about Texas."

Clay relaxed as he told them about the railroads

moving through Texas. He talked about reconstruction. Hack and his family were from Kentucky. They seemed to have northern sympathies.

They talked mainly of progress and westward movement.

And Hack told him he had lost a cousin at the Little Big Horn with Custer the previous year. He also talked about the third Kentucky Derby, held last May.

"Renshaw's Pride, he's gonna give us the right colt one of these days," Hack said. "We're gonna get that purse, you watch. This year, I read how the winner got thirty-three hundred dollars. He ran the mile and a half in two minutes and thirty-eight seconds. Why, when Renshaw's Pride was a colt, he coulda done that, but weren't no Derby then."

When supper was over, they retreated to sit around the hearth. Ladylike, Susanna left them alone.

"Tough land for women," Hack grunted. "Her ma died on the way here, so I sent Susanna back to St. Louis. And Tate Wiley's woman, why she ran off first month they were here. He ain't seen her since."

The conversation turned to horses and trail drives. Soon Clay picked up his hat, ready to leave.

Susanna appeared instantly. "Mr. Darringer, surely you will stay the night."

"No, thanks. The Turners were attacked last night. The bunkhouse was burned down. I'd better get back."

"How terrible," she said. "Was anyone hurt?"

"Not from the ranch. We hit a couple of 'em, but they were hauled off so we couldn't identify them."

The men didn't react to his news. Susanna walked him to the door and onto the porch. The lamplight came through the window onto her yellow hair. She stood close, smiling up at him.

"Will you be back?" she asked softly.

"Reckon not."

Anxious, she suddenly stepped forward, her hand on his arm. She stood on her tiptoes, waiting to be kissed, but Howie came to the doorway. She drew back. Clay was relieved.

"Please come back," she whispered.

Clay turned and went down the steps, hurrying to his roan in the darkness. He tightened the cinch, dropped the stirrup, and mounted. Then he tipped his hat at the lovely young woman.

As he rode away, he was again comparing her to Katherine. Both women were about twenty. Both were beautiful. But while Katherine was bold and outspoken, Susanna was peaceful and a lady. It would be easier to be around Susanna.

But he wanted to be free of them, to head for California. He thought of his wife. Her death and that of their unborn child had devastated him. No one would get that close to him again. Love made a man too vulnerable.

He was deep in thought as he rode away.

Susanna went back inside. She was still smiling to herself when her brother confronted her.

"Don't be wastin' yourself on a gunfighter."

"And who should I turn to?"

"Why not Jacob Turner?"

"He has no dash," she said, smiling.

"But he has the best ranch in this part of the country."

"Why, Howie. Would you marry your sister off just to get land?"

"You know blamed well I would."

"What's goin' on?" their father asked from his seat near the hearth. "Get over here and talk to me."

"Now, Pa," Howie said, "I was just tryin' to talk sense to your daughter."

"Well, who's gonna talk sense to you?" Hack growled. "You been spendin' too much time in gamblin' halls with women and cards."

"Now, Pa," Howie said, sitting opposite him, "you musta sowed a few wild oats."

"Maybe *I* would like to sow a few," Susanna told them.

"With Darringer?" Howie grunted.

"Why not?" she asked, smiling.

"Your sister's teasin' you," Hack said.

She came to sit on the arm of her father's chair, kissing his forehead. Howie crossed one leg over the other knee, leaning back with his hands behind his head.

"I can just see us now," Howie said. "With Susanna married to Jacob, why—"

"I will not marry Jacob Turner," she insisted.

"You have a stubborn streak," her father told her.

"Well, before long," Howie said, "there won't be no Turners left anyhow."

"You know somethin' I don't?" Hack questioned.

"Not a thing," Howie said, grinning.

"Howie enjoys being mysterious," Susanna chided.

"But really, Father, what's wrong with Clay Darringer?"

"He's a killer. You stay away from him."

Susanna merely smiled and kissed him again.

While the Renshaws were bantering with each other, Clay rode through the night, his thoughts troubled. Whoever was killing the Turners would not give up.

Back at the ranch, he came to the corrals, where Keyes was on guard.

The men had moved into the tack room and a nearby shed. They had already been at work rebuilding the bunkhouse.

Clay dismounted and unsaddled his horse, rubbing him down and walking him to cool him some before watering him. After he put him in the corral, he turned to Keyes, who was sitting on the fence in the moonlight.

"Any sign of trouble?" Clay asked.

"Been quiet," the young cowboy said. "Jacob's waitin' up for you."

"How's Perkins?"

"Mean as ever."

Clay grinned, taking up his Winchester. He walked to the high walls surrounding the ranch house. A grizzled cowhand let him in through the big gate. As he walked toward the house, he saw lights in the upstairs bedrooms. Entering, he found the lamps turned low and the fire burning bright in the hearth.

Jacob, who had been dozing in his chair fully clothed, looked up and rubbed his eyes. He leaned back, shoving the blankets down to his knees, looking relieved as Clay sat down near him.

"We were gettin' worried," Jacob said.

Jacob told him that Wes's hands were fine and remarked how brave the boy had been. He was already speaking of the youth as if he were a brother.

Clay told him about his visit to the Renshaws.

"Hack's a tough old buzzard," Jacob said. "If it was only him, I'd probably let him graze on my land. But then I'd have every other rancher pounding at the gate."

"You sleepin' down here?" Clay asked. Jacob nodded.

They talked awhile, then Clay said good night, moving wearily up the stairs, still carrying his Winchester. A lamp was hanging in the hallway, the chimney blackened by long use.

He passed three other doors before he reached the last one on the right. As he put his hand on the latch, he was stopped by a woman's voice.

"Clay, I'm glad you're back."

He turned, staring at Katherine as she approached from an open door. She was in a flowing blue dressing gown, with white lace at the collar. It made her look like a princess. Her red hair was soft on her shoulders. Her green eyes were glistening.

Holding his breath, he watched her come within inches. He looked down at her pretty face. He was getting uneasy.

"Good night," he said, about to open his door.

Her hand rested on his arm, stopping him. Her

touch went straight up to the back of his neck and down to his boots.

"Clay Darringer, you are not going to bed until you tell me about the Renshaws."

"Ask Jacob. I just filled him in."

"I don't want to hear man talk," she said firmly. "I want to know about Susanna."

Clay swallowed hard. "She was there."

"And she was very friendly."

"I reckon so."

Clay just couldn't deal with this woman. He opened the door to his room, trying to get away. She tugged at his arm. He stopped, looked down at her again.

Suddenly, she was on her toes, her soft hands at his face, pulling him down. Her velvet lips touched his rough mouth. He'd never been hit so hard in his life. The sensation went all the way through him. It was like being hit by dynamite all over again.

Transfixed, he had closed his eyes for only a moment when he felt her hands draw away. He looked down at her sweet, breathless smile. He was shaking in his boots as he backed away.

Escaping to his room, he quickly closed the door. Finally, he could breathe again. That woman scared him plenty. He could still taste the sweetness of her lips, and he wiped his mouth with the back of his hand. The taste didn't go away.

Sitting on the bed, he rubbed his still sore right shoulder and remembered Katherine's touch as she had massaged it with a firm hand.

He spent a restless night, and on Tuesday morning

he arose early. He went outside, joining the men for a sunrise breakfast in a shed before the Turners were awake.

"Tell Jacob I'm goin' to see Wiley," Clay told Perkins. "And I may stay in town a couple of nights."

"Well, be careful," the foreman said. "Now you see that there rock peak stickin' out of the hills, directly across the valley? Right below it's the Wiley ranch. But you oughta take a couple of men with you."

"Not lookin' for trouble. Best I go alone."

"Well, don't tell Miss Katherine I knowed you was goin'. She'd have my hide."

Clay was annoyed at the inference. He saddled his roan and swung astride. The foreman, hobbling with a pole for a crutch, came alongside.

"While you're in town, look around for a cook. We're gettin' tired o' our own fixin's. Our old one got scared off."

Perkins turned toward a far corral where a bronc was being tested. The foreman was too tough to let a bullet keep him down. Clay admired the man, as well as the loyal riders who stayed with the brand.

As he rode down the hillside, Clay glanced back at the homestead's walls, where the early light was now spreading. He knew he couldn't leave Castle Creek until the Turners were safe.

Also, he was concerned about the sheriff. This was only Tuesday. It was a long way to Friday, when the judge was to arrive.

He sighted the town within two hours, but kept riding.

Crossing Castle Creek, he saw the water swirling faster and deeper. Up north, he could see cattle at the banks. He headed east as the sun rose into his eyes.

By noon, he was only a couple of miles from the rock peak, where he could see Wiley cattle.

It was then that he was met by two riders. One of them was Riggs, the bearded foreman. The other was Tuck Wiley, still boyish and sloppy.

Despite his easy look, Tuck still had those dark, searing eyes. There was a short exchange about whether or not Clay could see Tate Wiley. At length, Tuck thought it would be fun and rode alone at his side toward the peak.

"You know, Darringer, just ridin' in here, you could be a dead man."

"That so?"

"Why, my old man eats fellas like you for breakfast."

"My hide's too tough."

"You funnin' me?"

Clay grinned, easing his roan around some rocks.

"Tuck, you remind me of an old cow got lost. You've got a lot of bellerin' in you."

"Takes a lot of guts to talk to me like that. You know, the Turners been gettin' cut down. How you know it wasn't me?"

"I figure even ambush is too dangerous for you."

Tuck spurred his horse and rode in front, turning to glare at him. Clay reined up. Tuck's searing eyes were shining like torches.

"Listen to me, Darringer, I ain't one bit afraid of you."

"That why you're bringin' in Carmody?"

Tuck spun his horse about, leading the way to the ranch, his hand resting on his holster all the while.

The ranch house was set in the trees, in the shadow of the high peak. Corrals and buildings were off to the right. Men came forward to watch as Tuck and Clay dismounted at the railing in front of the house.

Tuck led the way inside. It was a typical front room, with a fire in the hearth. The furniture was mostly leather. Hides hung on the wall.

Tuck yelled out for his father. From the back room, Tate Wiley appeared, tall and erect. Even in his ranch clothes, he looked like an officer. His long face was set in a polite smile. When Tuck introduced the visitor, his mouth went down at the corners.

"What do you want, Darringer?" Tate growled.

"I came to find out if you were the one having the Turners shot."

They stood facing each other in the big room. Tuck stood off to the side, staring. Tate was unarmed, but there was a Winchester over the hearth.

The rancher's face darkened with anger. "I don't fight like that," he growled.

"Your son Sheb around?"

"Sheb's been gone for months," Tuck cut in. "He's bringing in some cattle from Texas."

"With Turner cash?" Clay asked.

"What are you getting at?" Tate demanded.

"I reckon you haven't heard that Sid Turner and two of his men were murdered down in Bravo Canyon. His sister was left for dead."

"Listen to me," Tate said, "I'm a Texan, same as

you. I led my men with honor, and I haven't changed. I fight men head on, and I would never endanger a woman. Nor would my son."

"So you got no idea who's been ambushin' the Turners?"

"Darringer, you're trying my patience," the old man said. "Why don't you talk to the Renshaws?"

"I've been there. Renshaw claims he doesn't fight that way either."

"Well, every rancher in the valley wants that land. Any one of 'em could be tryin' the easy way. But come auction, it's the Wileys would be first in line."

"You're telling me," Clay said, "that in all these hills, you don't have enough grass and water of your own?"

"Darringer, I've got more land and less cattle than Turner. I have just enough feed and water to handle 'em. But I'm taking a chance with another five hundred."

"Sheb's bringing them in?" Clay asked. "I reckon that means you already got it figured where you're gonna spread 'em out."

"You don't make friends easy, do you?" Tate growled.

"Why don't we just shoot 'im?" Tuck suggested.

"Don't mind my son," Tate said. "He doesn't have my patience. Now you listen to me, Darringer. You got me painted like some tyrant. Fact is, I tried to buy Turner's ranch. Then I tried to buy water and grazin' rights. Nothing works with them."

"So you sent for Carmody," Clay surmised.

Tate's dark eyes narrowed. "I don't need anyone

to do my fighting for me. And you've overstayed your welcome."

Clay considered the man a moment longer. Then he turned and walked outside, a smirking Tuck following and watching him as he mounted his roan.

"You better start visitin' the other ranchers," Tuck said, sneering. "But maybe if you ask Carmody, he'll tell you who's payin' 'im."

"What about Thatcher?"

"Yeah, I heard about him," Tuck responded. "Guess they buried him yesterday. Poor old Thatch. Story is he lost at cards to Perkins and just plain went after 'im."

"Why did you fire him?"

"Truth is, he wasn't pullin' his load. We gave him a week's warnin' to see if he'd straighten out, but he got lazier than ever."

Clay studied Tuck for a long moment. Then he reined his horse to leave. The man called after him.

"You say hello to Miss Turner for me. Tell her I'll be callin'."

Disgusted, Clay rode all afternoon to get back to town, taking the long way to get a better view of the valley.

In town, he reined up in front of the sheriff's office and dismounted, draping the reins over the railing. The wall had been repaired. New timber surrounded the doorframe.

He paused to look up and down the street. It was all normal. Wagons, dogs, children, horses. Old-timers were sitting in the shade.

Entering, he found Cox tacking up a new poster.

The lawman looked glad to see him. They sat down, Cox behind his desk. The cells were empty.

"You look all right," Clay said.

"Thanks to you."

"How's Thatcher?"

"Had a funeral yesterday," Cox said. "Got him down in the storeroom at the mercantile. He's plenty scared."

Clay told him about his visits to Renshaw and Wiley.

"Well, I don't trust any of 'em," Cox said.

"What are you plannin' to do about Carmody?"

"You gettin' nervous?" Cox asked, grinning. "Well, fact is, only time you see 'im is when he's gambling."

"I figure on stayin' in town a few days, till Friday."

"I'd be plenty glad to see you on Friday, but not afore. Not with Carmody around."

"Believe me, it's safer in town."

Cox grinned. "You got woman trouble?"

"Two of 'em. I was over to Renshaw's."

"Now, Susanna, she's a real fine lady."

"Maybe, but they both scare me plenty. I'd sooner wrestle a bear."

"With fifty bachelors to every single woman," Cox said, "I can't figure what they see in you."

"Well, I reckon Katherine's just a little loco. And Susanna, she probably thinks she can make a gentleman out of me."

"Yeah, women do like serious projects."

Cox finally persuaded Clay to head back to the ranch. He didn't want any street fighting in his town, at least not until after Thatcher's trial. He advised him to check at the mercantile for a cook. But first, he and Clay had supper at the hotel.

Unable to find an available cook, Clay mounted his roan and headed back toward the ranch.

It was a starry night. He enjoyed the cool darkness.

At the ranch, he unsaddled his roan at the corral, told Perkins there was no cook in town, and headed reluctantly toward the walled ranch house. If he was lucky, Katherine would already be sound asleep.

Keyes was at the gate and let him inside. The young cowhand was grinning.

"Guess what?" he asked as he closed the gate.

"I'm in no mood for games."

"We got company. Miss Renshaw."

Clay paused, looking toward the house. The lamps were all turned up high. He would have trouble sneaking to his room for a good night's sleep. Ill at ease, he went in the front door.

Seated around the hearth were Jacob, Katherine, Wes, and Susanna. Clay's face went hot. He looked from one smiling woman to the other. He reluctantly took the chair Wes pulled up for him.

Katherine was wearing a blue silk dress with blue lace. Her guest was wearing her riding clothes, topped by a green velvet jacket and little feathered hat. Both were sitting on the sofa.

"Susanna came too late to go home," Katherine explained.

"Unless you would like to escort me back," Susanna said to Clay.

There was a long, dangerous silence. Clay

shrugged and shook his head, looking at Jacob, who was only grinning. The women were both smiling politely. Wes, his hands bandaged, saved the moment.

"Did you really ride to the Wileys'?" Wes asked.

Clay nodded, relating the story of his visit. "I can't figure it," he said. "I don't see Tate Wiley as a back shooter. I'm not so sure about his son Tuck. Sheb's supposed to have been gone for several months, bringing in more cattle."

"And what about my father?" Susanna asked. "Do you suspect him?"

"No, I don't reckon he'd pull an ambush," Clay told her, "but I'm not too sure about your brother."

Susanna's smile faded. "I'd like to talk to you, Clay. Outside, in the garden."

"It's cold out there," Katherine said quickly. "And I've already told you, he works for us."

"This is rather personal," Susanna retorted.

"Not safe out there," Clay said, trembling in his boots. He was not about to get out in the darkness with either one of these women. "Besides, I'm turning in."

"I think I will too," Katherine added.

"So will I," Susanna chimed in rather quickly.

"On the other hand," Clay said, "if you ladies want to turn in, I've got business to talk with Jacob."

"I own half this ranch," Katherine reminded him. "You can talk to me as well."

"This is man's talk," Jacob said, obviously feeling sorry for Clay. "You ladies go on upstairs."

"I declare," Susanna said, rising prettily. "You men are living in the dark ages."

Clay watched them up the stairs and out of sight, then drew a deep breath. Wes was grinning broadly.

Jacob laughed. "You've got a problem there."

"Susanna's family know she's here?"

"No, she told 'em she was spendin' the night in town with friends. She said she wanted to see Katherine without being told she couldn't. But I don't think she came to see Katherine."

Clay leaned back, frustrated over his woman problem, but he finally relaxed. Wes, weary from a day's work, left them and went upstairs. Clay related Tate's arguments.

"I gotta protect my cattle," Jacob said. "All they gotta do is not overstock and they'll make out fine. Ain't my fault Tate's got more cattle comin'. He probably gets only seven or eight acres per steer on that sandy ground. Over here, we got the river valley with rich soil, and so much grass that we can handle one steer every four acres."

"Well, you'd better watch yourself."

"With all that's goin' on around here, I wouldn't blame you if you left. You know Carmody'll wanta build his reputation on you. If Thatcher gets to trial, he's liable to talk plenty to save his neck, and that could mean trouble. If Sheb shows up, we gotta have him arrested. And I'm not sure we can stand another attack on the ranch."

"You're mighty long-winded," Clay said, grinning. "First off, there'd be only one reason for me to light out, and that's all female."

"So you're staying?"

"I don't have any choice."

"You're more man than most, Clay Darringer. You have my respect. And I sure thank you for bein' here."

Clay nodded, a little embarrassed. He wanted to explain that not one of his brothers would ride away when friends were in trouble. Nor would a Darringer turn his back on a lawman in need of help. It was not a matter of choice.

"Well," Clay said, "since Sheb was on the trail comin' up from Texas, who do you suppose shot you?"

"Take your pick."

Clay shrugged. After some further discussion, he said good night and headed quietly up the stairs, then walked as softly as he could down the hallway. He saw lights under Katherine's door as he passed. Nervously, he made it to his room and latched the door safely.

With relief, he lay back on the soft bed, falling asleep before he could undress. His slumber was restless, and he tossed about, dreaming. He could see his wife's face, sweet and smiling. He saw men he had fought in dusty streets. Sometimes, he saw his brothers.

When he awakened late in the night, he saw nothing but darkness.

But he smelled smoke—coming in under the door!

Chapter Seven

*C*lay sprang from his bed. The smoke was curling under the door. The ceiling was red-hot. Still dressed, he had only to pull on his hat, holster his six-gun, and take up his Winchester. He paused to turn up the lamp, glancing behind him at the window.

He knew he could get out alone, but he never hesitated.

Reaching the door, he felt the wood. It was hot, but he couldn't stop. He knelt and drew it open. Smoke was heavy in the hallway but it was mostly high in the air, clinging to the hot ceiling. He dropped to his knees.

He heard Jacob yelling at the top of the stairs.

"Katherine! Susanna! Wes! Clay, where are you?"

Across from Clay, Wes came out of his smoke-filled room, instantly coughing. He knelt, carrying his boots as he crawled toward Clay. He was shirtless but wearing his britches.

"Get out my window," Clay hollered. "We'll get the women."

The youth started to argue, but he was now coughing badly. He took Clay's Winchester and crawled past the gunfighter to continue toward the window, Clay pulled his bandanna over his mouth and nose, rising to a bent position.

As Clay hurried up the hallway toward Jacob's loud voice, he heard the window glass being smashed behind him in his room. It was getting hard to breathe, but Clay continued until he saw Jacob crawling to Katherine's door on Clay's left. He dropped down on his hands and knees.

"They're both in here," Jacob said, coughing.

The door was locked. Jacob was fully dressed, as that was the way he usually slept in the chair; he was still on his knees and pounding the door with his fists. Clay came to his side. They could see smoke curling up from under the door. They could be too late.

With a silent roar, Clay got to his feet and backed away, charging with his left shoulder, slamming against the door several times. Jacob struggled to stand and kick at the latch as Clay kept striking the frame.

Abruptly, the door broke open. The smoke was so thick that they had to back away and get down on their hands and knees, crawling through the darkness. The only light was from the red-hot ceiling. It was a furnace, airless and suffocating.

Each man found a side of the bed and grabbed a female body. They took blankets and each rolled his charge into one. The women were limp, barely struggling, coughing and fighting for air. Jacob tried to open the window, without success.

A woman in his arms, Clay rose and kicked at the

window until the glass shattered. He knew it was a fifteen-foot drop.

Hesitant, he turned to Jacob.

"Toss 'em down to me," he said, setting his charge against the wall. He then climbed through the broken window and jumped.

The ground came up to meet him like a hammer. He landed on his feet but felt his body shudder in pain all the way to his hat. He dropped to his knees momentarily but recovered, pulling his bandanna from his face. He stood waiting, arms outstretched.

The roof was a roaring fire. Black smoke filled the cold night air. Sick at the sight, he waited, terrified that Jacob was gone, that all three were overcome.

Then he saw a blanket-bound female being thrust through the window's broken frame. He sprang forward, catching her in his arms. His right shoulder screamed with shock. As he turned, he saw Wes rushing to his aid. He shoved the woman, Susanna, he thought, into Wes's arms.

Another body came flying down toward Clay. He reached up, better at it this time, catching the woman and swinging about to break the fall. There was no shoulder pain.

The sudden flareup of flames along the wall threw light on his burden. It was Katherine, red hair spilling about her face, eyes closed as she lay in his arms, still fighting to breathe. She reached up to grab his shirt, holding on tightly.

Now Jacob was getting out, just in time. The roar of the roof falling was like thunder, chasing him out the window. He fell crazily but landed on his feet, then dropped to his knees.

"Let's get outa here," Jacob shouted, coughing as he took Susanna from Wes's arms. His eyes were running with tears from the smoke.

Wes picked up the Winchester he had abandoned to help Clay, and led the way around the house. "They killed the two guards," he said. "Knifed 'em. Somehow they got over the wall."

"Consarn it," Jacob muttered.

In front and away from the house, they moved back into the garden to get a good look at the destruction on the roof. The fire was wild, licking the timber and crawling down the walls. They could hear crashes inside as parts of the roof caved in. Heat reached them even as they backed away.

Perkins and his other six men came charging through the gate. Two set about pumping water from the well and passing out buckets, but it was too late. They began to try to save the surrounding wall.

The women were laid down near the well, one hundred feet away from the house and nearer to the outside wall. They were still coughing, gasping for air, clutching their throats. Both wore white, lace-trimmed gowns under their blankets.

Jacob laid Susanna out on the grass, slapping her face gently. Her head rolled to one side, even as she tried to take in the night air. He shook her, frantic. She began to breathe. She reached up and clutched his arms.

"Jacob," Susanna managed to whisper.

Clay knelt over Katherine, who was looking at him

now as she fought for air. He knew somehow he had to get fresh air into her lungs. He bent close and blew on her face, into her nostrils.

She gasped, trying to speak. He pressed down into her diaphragm. She coughed. Wide-eyed, she gazed up at him. He decided to try something else and bent down, putting his mouth over hers, blowing into her lungs.

He felt her body rise beneath him. He drew back.

She was coughing again, but not as painfully, and she was calmer now, staring up at him as tears filled her eyes and trickled down her face.

"I'm all right," she gasped.

He sat on his heels and looked over at Susanna. She was sitting up, Jacob pulling the blanket back around her. She was nodding her thanks.

Katherine was trying to sit up now, and Clay took her arm, helping her. He drew the blanket up around her. He and Jacob used their bandannas to wash and cool the women's faces.

They watched the men backing away from the flaming house. It was no use. They had to get out of the garden.

Jacob swung Susanna up in his arms. She slid her hand up his chest, resting her face against him. He hurried toward the gate.

Katherine was lifted into Clay's embrace. She settled against him as he walked, then ran, to follow Jacob.

They were all outside now: Wes, Perkins, his six men, and Jacob and Clay with their burdens.

The only decent shelter left was the tack room, which had been converted to a temporary bunkhouse.

Inside, by the lantern light, the women were settled onto the nearest bunks. The men gathered around, offering strong coffee and hard bread. The women, still suffering discomfort from the smoke inhalation, accepted only coffee. Wes chewed on the bread.

Sitting side by side, Susanna and Katherine were shivering. More blankets were spread over them.

"Thank you," Susanna said to a hairy cowhand who was spreading another blanket to cover their feet.

The room was crowded with gear. The walls were covered with bridles, hats, and hides. In a far corner, the saddles were crowded against the wall. The make-shift bunks were almost side by side.

"Well, the house is gone," Jacob said.

"We'll build another," Katherine murmured. She looked at Clay, her green eyes shining. "Thank you."

"You're a lot of trouble," Clay said awkwardly.

"And you're hard as a rock," Susanna put in, smiling. "You broke every bone in my body when you caught me."

"You look all right," Jacob told her.

"Shall we go into town?" Katherine asked, looking down at her white cotton nightgown as she tugged the blanket around her.

"No, we'll go to my place," Susanna said. "My clothes will fit you. Clay, you and Jacob are also welcome. And Wes, if he likes."

"I'll hitch up a wagon," Perkins volunteered.

Someone gave Wes a shirt to wear. He donned it,

sitting on a bunk and wiping ash from his face. He told them he had decided to stay on the ranch and sleep in the tack room.

Perkins and several of the men went outside to get the wagon. Clay followed, arranging for his roan and another horse to be saddled.

When the wagon was ready, the women climbed in and were covered with more blankets. For a moment, everyone paused to stare at the flames shooting above the walls surrounding the house. They lit up the sky.

Clay mounted his roan. Jacob's bay was tied behind the wagon bed. Jacob climbed onto the wagon seat, taking up the reins.

Riding ahead of the wagon, Clay thought angrily of what was happening to the Turners. Someone wanted all the Turners dead.

Maybe the Wileys. Tate was a martinet, too proud for ambush, but his son Tuck—and maybe Sheb—was not that particular.

Or the Renshaws. Hack had sounded square, but he, too, wanted to build his herd. His son Howie was certainly capable of anything.

Or it could be any of the other ranchers Clay had not met.

And there was the question of who hired Thatcher to shoot Perkins. The other serious question was, Who sent for Carmody?

The ride through the dark, cold night often gave them glimpses of the last flames at the ranch house. The brightness had fallen away to a glow. Now it was easier to see the stars in the black sky.

In the wagon bed, the women huddled together.

It was several hours before they crossed enough wooded hills to reach the wire fence. Jacob climbed down and snipped it with cutters that had been in the wagon. They drove through, the team picking its way.

They turned and headed west through the trees, climbing now. At length, they were going downhill toward the Renshaw spread.

A nighthawk suddenly flew up, startling the team. Jacob calmed them and drove onward.

Two men came to meet them at the corrals. One helped with the horses while the other went to awaken the Renshaws.

Howie and Hack came outside just as Jacob and Clay lifted the women from the back of the wagon. Hack hurried to his daughter, taking her from Jacob's arms. Howie tried to take Katherine, but she clung to Clay, her face buried in his shirt.

Inside the house, a fire was burning brightly in the hearth. The women were settled on the sofa. The Mexican woman appeared and went to the iron stove in the back room to heat up the coffee. Hack sat near his daughter. He was anxious.

"Susanna, are you all right? What happened?"

"Some men burned the Turner house. I was staying there."

"We thought you were in town," Hack said.

"I changed my mind. And I've asked Katherine and Jacob and Clay to stay with us," she told him.

"Well, sure," her father agreed.

"Thanks," Jacob said. "But Clay and I'll just stay

the night. I would appreciate it, though, if Katherine could stay a few days."

"She can stay as long as she likes," Hack offered. "We got plenty of room."

The Mexican woman brought the coffee. Howie, his blue eyes narrowed and surrounded by crinkled skin, kept looking at Katherine in the blanket. He seemed to have less than the honorable intentions he had previously avowed.

His attention irritated Clay, who was seated in a chair near the couch. He looked at Jacob, who also had noticed Howie's new interest.

"As I think about it," Jacob said abruptly, "I think Katherine should move into the hotel. We'll take her there tomorrow."

"Might not be safe," Hack warned.

"No reason she can't stay here," Howie said.

"I'd like the company," Susanna added.

Katherine took the signals from her brother and Clay.

"No, thanks," she said, smiling at Susanna. "But I would appreciate something to wear into town."

The women decided to go upstairs to bathe and retire. Blankets wrapped around them, they walked barefoot to the far stairway, where they paused. They smiled back at Jacob and Clay, then went up the steps with the Mexican woman following.

"Brave women," Hack said, after a long moment.

"Your daughter grow up here?" Clay asked.

"Nope, she lived most of her life in St. Louis," the rancher said. "She's a real lady, too refined for the men in this valley. May have to send her back."

After more of the heavy coffee, Clay and Jacob retired to an empty room at the head of the stairs. There were two bunks and miscellaneous bridles and harness.

Jacob turned up the lamp and flopped on a bunk.

"I tell you, Clay, I can't take much more of this. How can you fight an enemy you can't see?"

"I don't know."

"What are you going to do about Thatcher?"

"I'll be spending a couple of nights in town," Clay said.

"Well, seein' as the judge comes on Friday, and I haven't got a house, I think I'll just stay in town myself. It'll give me a chance to keep an eye on Katherine."

Weary, the men turned in for the night.

Wednesday morning's breakfast was hot and tasty, served by the Mexican woman. Clay began to wonder if Susanna could cook. Then, observing how lovely she was, he decided it didn't matter.

Later they sat around the fire, the men telling stories. The women sat on the sofa.

Katherine was wearing a green dress that matched her eyes. It was a bit long, as Susanna was taller, but it fit her well. Her red hair spread in soft waves on her shoulders. Her hostess was wearing a calico print, her hair again done up in pretty curls.

It startled Clay to think that after the fire and coming so near death, Susanna had spent time before bed setting curls in her hair. Then he smiled. He kind of liked that.

Howie was always leering at Katherine. Clay

didn't like that. Nor did Jacob. Howie Renshaw and Tuck Wiley could have been brothers, the way they acted around women.

"We oughta be gettin' on into town," Jacob said.

"Well, I sure hope you find out who's trying to kill you off," Hack grunted.

"Could be anybody," Jacob remarked. "Could be you."

"Why, Jacob Turner," Susanna said, frowning prettily.

"It's all right, honey," her father told her. "Jacob's got a right to question everybody."

"We think Sheb Wiley was one of the killers," Jacob said.

Clay looked at Howie Renshaw. "You been ridin' south?"

Hack took offense. Howie merely grinned.

"I hear you're kind of fast with that gun," Clay told Howie. "Doc told me you shot his son two years ago."

Howie's smile turned to a sneer. "It was a fair fight, and Doc's son was cheatin' at cards. Ask anybody."

Clay wasn't impressed. The others tried to relieve the tension with small talk. The conversation returned to the Friday arrival of the circuit judge.

"Well, if Thatcher had lived, the trial would have been mighty interestin'," Hack noted.

"I've never seen a trial," Susanna said.

"Wouldn't have been a fancy trial like you mighta seen in St. Louis. Got no fool lawyers here. Just a travelin' judge."

"I met a nice lawyer in St. Louis," Susanna remembered wistfully. "He wanted to marry me."

"I'd as soon have you marry a Wiley," the rancher grunted.

"My brother's a lawyer," Clay said. "A fine, honest lawyer."

Renshaw grinned. "Sorry, Clay."

When Clay and Jacob asked for the wagon, Howie went out to see that the team was harnessed. Susanna insisted on giving Katherine a carpetbag full of clothing to help her until she could do some shopping at the stores in town.

Out in the fresh morning air, Katherine climbed onto the wagon seat with Jacob, whose bay was again tied behind. Clay mounted his roan. The carpetbag was tossed in the wagon bed with the blankets the Turners had brought with them.

Susanna came to Clay's side, smiling up at him. She put her hand on his boot as she spoke.

"Thank you again, Clay Darringer, and you too, Jacob."

Jacob nodded his response, hesitating long enough to drink in how pretty she was. Then he took up the reins, released the foot brake, and turned the wagon.

They moved away from the Renshaw ranch house, into the hills and woods. The sun was hazy. Clouds were moving overhead.

After they went through the cut fence, they headed around by way of the Turner ranch. The house was gone entirely. Nothing was standing except the fortress walls. Perkins came up to greet them. He told them that the two guards had been buried on a nearby hill.

Katherine sat quietly on the wagon seat, not wanting to see. Perkins joined Clay and Jacob as they went inside the walls. Jacob stood transfixed, staring at the ashes and fireplace.

"Well, we got no ranch house and only six men left," Perkins said gruffly.

"We'll rebuild," Jacob promised. "May have to sell a few cattle."

"We already sold the Army everything they need right now," Perkins pointed out. "With the Apache headin' south, the reservations aren't gonna be as hungry."

"We'll round 'em up in the spring," Jacob said. "If we have to, we'll take 'em to Wyoming. But we're gonna start rebuilding now. My credit's good."

Perkins and Clay were silent, both knowing Jacob was asking for a lot. The bunkhouse was only beginning to be rebuilt. Only Perkins and six hands remained until roundup. Meanwhile, the Turners were still in danger.

But on Friday, Clay thought, Thatcher could well shoot off his mouth as to who had hired him. He turned to Perkins.

"You ever play cards with Thatcher?"

The foreman grinned. "Sure did. I beat him every time."

"You make fun of him?" Clay persisted.

"Well, I guess I did. Made him awful mad."

"Then you'd better come to town early Friday,"

Jacob said. "Man oughta have a fair trial. But keep it quiet that he's still alive."

Perkins nodded agreement.

With a last look at the remains of his home, Jacob led the way out of the garden, through the gates. It was still mid-morning and plenty cold.

"Winter's comin' fast," Perkins remarked.

Back on the wagon, Jacob turned the team toward town. It already looked like rain. The dark clouds were moving in from the northwest. The sun was often shut out by drifting white clouds.

Before noon, they were on the last rise, moving down through the aspens toward the distant town. It was already sprinkling.

As they neared Castle Creek and the road into town, they saw Sheriff Cox riding north. He had on his slicker and was riding a big sorrel.

Cox reined up alongside the wagon and tipped his hat to Katherine. Jacob told him about the fire, and asked about Thatcher.

"We got him hidden away," Cox said. "Simon, the blacksmith, is keepin' an eye on 'im. So far, we've kept the secret pretty well."

"We'll be careful," Jacob promised.

"Right now, I could use Clay's help," Cox said.

Clay told the others to continue into town, and he rode along the creek with the lawman, heading north. It was raining now. Clay pulled on his slicker.

"You're not even goin' to ask me what I want?" Cox asked.

"I figured you'd tell me sooner or later."

Cox reined up opposite the distant rock peak that

marked the Wiley spread. He pointed to some rugged cliffs farther back and to the northeast as he spoke.

"Up there's a Wiley line shack. Last night, old Thatcher got to worryin' about Yuma and the Snake Den. He can't stand confinement, you know. So I told 'im I'd recommend a light sentence if he'd do some talking."

"So we're goin' after Sheb Wiley."

"You figured it. Last Friday night, Sheb got to the ranch late. Well, seems like Thatcher was out for a smoke and overheard Sheb and a Shanty Wells man talkin' plenty. Next evenin', reckon Sheb found out Miss Turner was still alive and took off for the line shack."

"You figure he's alone?"

"Thatcher said the fellas Sheb brought with him from Texas got scared and took off. But I ain't sure if any of the Shanty Wells men are there."

"So two of us might not be enough."

"You worried?" Cox asked, grinning.

Clay just shrugged and followed him along the creek. The rain was heavier, pouring down their slickers. Their mounts started sliding now and then in the mud. The creek was rising.

Soon they crossed over to the east side and started cutting across the valley floor, aiming for the distant cliffs. It was early afternoon when they started climbing through the rocks and brush.

The rain was shooting streams in every direction. The sky had darkened so much that they forgot it was daylight. Only an occasional flash of lightning brought clear vision.

At length, they were riding through a narrow canyon.

"Wiley don't use this line shack 'cept for huntin'," Cox remarked. "He built it when he was plannin' to buy out half the valley. His plans got waylaid when the Turners refused to sell at any price."

Now they saw the timber shack sitting on a rise near a high bluff. In the dark rain, they could see a lamp burning through the cracks around the shuttered window. In a nearby lean-to, there was only one horse, a black gelding with white stockings.

"Maybe we'll be lucky," Cox said.

They dismounted and crept up to the shack. Clay peered in the window. Only Sheb Wiley was there, stretched out on a bunk, tossing cards into his hat. He looked like an older Tuck, having the same boyish face. The door was barred.

Together, Clay and Cox picked up an uncut log near the woodpile. Gripping it, they charged the door. As the log slammed into the latch side, the door gave way with a loud wrench.

Sheb sprang to his feet, pulling his gun, just as Clay reached him and slammed his fist into the boyish face.

Sheb fought for balance. Clay hit him again, then grabbed Sheb's gun as the man fell to the floor.

"What the devil are you doin' here?" Sheb snarled.

"You're under arrest," Cox said, six-gun in hand.

"What for?" Sheb demanded, getting to his feet.

"For killin' Sid Turner and two cowhands," the lawman said. "And for tryin' to kill Miss Turner."

Clay spun the man around so Cox could handcuff

his hands behind his back. Clay shoved Sheb's hat on his head and hung a slicker around him.

There were signs in the cabin indicating that other men had been sleeping there. Some gear was still stashed in the corners. Bottles of whiskey and some empty cups sat on the small table.

Sheb was hastily dragged outside. His horse was saddled, and he was unceremoniously hoisted astride. Clay shoved the reins between Sheb's teeth.

The three, mounted in the rain, headed back down the canyon. With luck, they would not be seen.

They crossed the valley floor, skirted some huddled cattle, forded the now racing creek, and headed for town. It was already nightfall.

The town seemed empty. Some horses stood in the rain with their heads down. A dog cowered under the boardwalk near the hotel. The men reined up in front of the jail, dismounting to enter. Water drained from their slickers onto the hardwood floor.

Sheb was shoved into a cell, his hands freed, and the door of steel bars slammed in his face. Sheb had the same dark, searing eyes as his younger brother. He glared at them with defiance.

"My Pa finds out, this place won't hold me," Sheb snarled.

Cox ignored him and turned to Clay. "You go ahead and eat. Then bring me some supper. I'll have to share what I get with Sheb. No use spreadin' the word so quick."

"Sheb's right, you know," Clay said. "When Tate Wiley finds out, he'll come tearin' in here."

"Likely he won't find out that quick," Cox told

him. "Depends if anyone rides on up to the line shack."

Clay shrugged and went outside. He hunched over in the cold rain and hurried up the steps of the hotel. Inside, he saw Katherine and Jacob about to walk into the dining room.

Clay removed his slicker and joined them, taking time to order food for the lawman. Katherine was still wearing Susanna's dress.

They all had something to eat. The stooped waiter brought them more coffee when they had finished.

"We got Sheb Wiley," Clay murmured. "But we gotta keep it quiet as long as we can."

Katherine looked stricken with sudden fear. It was as if she were back in the canyon. Her hands were trembling as she sipped her coffee, staring down at the steam.

"And he'll stand trial?" Jacob asked.

"Since the judge is comin'," Clay said, "might as well give it a try. If Katherine's willin' to testify."

"But if Wiley gets off," Jacob pointed out, "she'd be in worse danger."

"I'm not afraid," she said, no color in her face.

"Who's the judge?" Clay asked.

"Peabody," Jacob said. "He's a fair man."

As the conversation centered around the Turner murders, Clay watched Katherine with admiration as she recovered.

After all she'd been through, there she sat with the same bravado, bound and determined to set things right, even if it meant her life. He thought again that she had more courage than she could handle. But he also knew the mind was a fragile thing when it came to trauma. He was worried.

They discussed Perkins's admission that he had been beating Thatcher at cards and making fun of the big man. There was much speculation as to what would happen on Friday.

"Where's Carmody?" Clay asked finally.

"Playin' cards, mostly," Jacob said. "I'm told Howie's been comin' to town 'most every night to try to beat him. Howie doesn't like to lose at anything."

Clay returned to the jail with a tray of food. He spent the night there with Cox, taking turns on guard. Before daybreak, he walked down in the rain to check on Thatcher.

At first light, since there was no sign of Tate Wiley, Clay had breakfast at the hotel, ordering food for Cox and the prisoner at the same time. He went to the barber's for a shave. Refreshed, he went to the mercantile again to check on Thatcher, who was still hidden in the storeroom.

Then he started up the street toward the jail. The rain had stopped. Sunlight occasionally broke through the dark clouds.

He saw Katherine and Jacob on the porch steps. He crossed over to join them. She wore a borrowed slicker. Her red hair was fluffy about her face and shoulders.

The street was muddy, and no boards had been laid across. Katherine looked shyly at Clay.

"Jacob's going to the doctor," she said. "Would you help me to the store?"

Jacob grinned. "I guess it's no fun to be carried by your brother."

Uneasy, Clay hesitated. He had held her in his arms more than once. He had cared for her when she was out of her mind. Just the other night, he had carried her from a burning house. He had breathed life into her, his lips covering hers.

He thought of the kiss she had given him at her house.

There was no way he was going to pick her up now.

But there she was, moving in front of him, arms lifted, smiling at him as if he had no choice. He looked helplessly at Jacob.

"Go ahead," Jacob said, still grinning.

With a deep breath, Clay looked down at Katherine's demure smile.

This was a bold, forward woman. Yet at this moment she was fragile and feminine. He just couldn't handle that mixture. At least Susanna was only one person.

Katherine reached up and put her left hand on his right shoulder. She smelled of lilacs. He swallowed hard. Despite himself, he reached down and lifted her into his arms. Her gentle weight didn't bother his shoulder. Her soft dress and the harsh slicker rustled different tunes.

She was light, trim, beautiful. He refused to look down at her as he carried her across the street.

His boots kept sticking in the mud as he struggled to get to the other side. He could see Jacob heading down to the doctor's office over the mercantile. He followed in a haphazard fashion.

"Your brother all right?" he asked her.

"He had some pain, that's all."

"He had a rough night at the house."

"So did you. You saved me again, Clay."

"That don't mean nothing."

"There's an old saying that if you save someone's life, you have to take care of them," she told him playfully.

"You made that up."

He looked down at her silly smile and knew he was right. Her shining green eyes were filled with affection. He swallowed hard and set her down on the boardwalk as fast as he could. He backed away as if she were a rattlesnake.

"Aren't you coming in to help me?" she asked.

"Your brother will be down from the doc soon."

"Clay, are you afraid of me?"

"You bet," he said, his face hot.

She smiled, dimples dancing, reaching toward him.

Exasperated, he spun on his heel and headed back across the street, fighting the mud all the harder to vent his frustration. He walked into the Wiley hangout. The saloon was nearly empty, except for the bartender and a man at the bar.

Clay didn't want anything to drink. He just wanted to refresh his memory of the scene where they had caught Thatcher.

Unfortunately, the man at the bar was Carmody.

Turning to look at Clay, his thin black mustache curling up with his mouth at one corner, Carmody acted pleased to see him. Still in black and decorated with silver conchos, Carmody was more of a play-actor. He was trying to build a reputation that included his trademark apparel. But there was nothing false about the six-guns he wore.

Clay leaned on the bar, shaking his head at the bald, nervous barkeep.

"Just looking around," Clay said.

"I'm disappointed," Carmody countered. "I thought you were looking for me."

"Not a chance," Clay said.

"You know I won't be leavin' town until we finish, you and I."

"Just why *are* you in town?" Clay asked, ignoring the subtle challenge.

Carmody smiled, his mouth still curved up on one side. "Just travelin' through," he replied. "Wanted to see what Castle Creek was like. Now that you're here, I'm in no hurry to leave."

"I got no reason to fight you, Carmody."

"Maybe we can find one. What about Miss Turner?"

"She wouldn't have nothin' to do with you. And her brother would have something to say about it."

"From what I've seen," the gunman said, "she has a mind of her own. But I also noticed how you got mighty irritated whenever I fancied up to her."

"Just don't like your kind."

"And what kind are you?"

Clay drew a deep breath. He didn't want to fight this man, verbally or otherwise. He shrugged and turned, leaving the saloon and walking up the street.

The sky was clearing rapidly. But his mind wasn't. He kept hearing Carmody's last question.

Maybe even Clay didn't know what kind of a man he was. He had thought to be a doctor, but his grand theory of perfection in medicine and helping others hadn't held up when his wife died.

Clay was a fast gun, all right, but he had no need to kill anyone. The only homes he had known were with his wife, so briefly, and with his brothers in Texas. He was proud of his brothers, loved them, and wanted to see them, but each had his own life.

He had liked being a tracker and scout for the Army. He was good at it. No tiny stone rolled out of its earth socket had ever escaped his eye. Matching wits with the equally cunning Apache had made for respect on both sides. But he had been restless and moved on.

He still wanted to go to California, but once he got there, he would be alone. He would be a man without a star. Even the thought of owning his own spread reminded him that he would be alone in whatever house he built.

No, he didn't know what kind of man he was. Maybe he never would. And the thought was mighty unsettling.

As he started up the boardwalk toward the hotel, he saw Howie Renshaw riding into town on a sorrel gelding. Renshaw reined up in front of the saloon where Clay was standing.

Howie dismounted, wrapping the reins about the hitching rail. His crooked, lean face was set with a smile. "Well, Darringer, are you lookin' for a card game?"

"Not a chance."

"Carmody in there?"

"Yes, but you'd better watch yourself."

"You figure I can't handle him?" Howie asked, grinning.

"You may be fast, but you don't realize the kind of man he is."

"And what kind is that?"

"He's not afraid to die."

Howie just laughed and walked past him into the saloon.

Clay shrugged and walked toward the hotel. Across the street, he saw Katherine and her brother coming out with a lot of bundles. She saw Clay and called to him for help.

Clay reluctantly admitted to himself that Jacob couldn't carry her as well as the bundles. He nodded and crossed over.

"How did you do with the doc?" Clay asked Jacob.

"He said I just hadn't used a few muscles for a time. He wants me to stop sittin' by the fire and start workin'."

"You figure he sent for Carmody?" Clay asked.

Jacob and Katherine looked distressed.

"Everyone likes ole Doc," Jacob said quietly. "If you're thinkin' he's got Carmody here to take care of Howie, you better not be sayin' it."

"He said Howie killed his only son," Clay reminded him.

"That's true, but his son wasn't worth much anyhow."

"What's a man's life worth?" Clay asked.

"Forget it," Jacob snapped. "Carmody's here to kill Turners, nothing more."

"Stop this," Katherine said firmly. "Clay Darringer, you have two empty arms there."

He looked down at her in the sunlight. She was beautiful, her red hair darkened, her green eyes shining.

Despite his fierce reluctance, he had to pick her up again. She settled in his arms, smiling at him. Grimacing, he started across the street, a grinning Jacob following with her purchases.

Clay moved as fast as he could. He hadn't reached the other boardwalk when they heard a yell. He paused in the middle of the street. Slowly, Clay turned, Katherine balanced in his arms.

Jacob was at his side. All three looked toward the saloon as Howie Renshaw came storming outside.

"Get out here, Carmody," Howie was yelling over his shoulder.

The expected audience came out of doorways. Cox came out of the jail.

Howie stomped into the muddy street.

Chapter Eight

*H*owie stood in the muddy street in the afternoon sun. There was a long wait. Carmody took his time. He was a showman. He moved through the swinging doors and stood on the boardwalk, his silver conchos gleaming.

Howie had backed twenty feet away, his back to Clay and the Turners, who were still crossing the street. Hurriedly, Clay stumbled over to the boardwalk and set Katherine down.

"Get to the hotel, both of you," Clay ordered.

"What are you going to do?" she asked.

"Nothing. Just do as I say."

"You're terribly bossy," she said, miffed.

Jacob stepped in, carrying the bundles and guiding her away from the trouble. Clay waited until they were on the steps and entering the hotel. He turned, watching the spectators moving back to safety and windows.

Clay looked over at Cox, then at the mercantile and the second story. Framed in the window was the old doctor.

There was no doubt that it would be a fair fight. Carmody's reputation was at stake.

The gunman moved into the street, facing Howie. They remained twenty feet apart. Carmody seemed annoyed because he was getting his boots muddy.

"What's your problem, son?" the gunman asked.

"You were dealin' off the bottom," Howie said loudly.

"Any witnesses?"

"Just you and me, Carmody. I aim to set it straight."

"I'm a lot faster than you, son."

"Stop callin' me son," Howie snarled.

"Where do you want it? In the heart?"

"You're gettin' it first, so don't you be makin' any plans."

The two men faced each other. The spectators crowded windows and doorways. The doctor was still at his window above the mercantile. Cox moved along the sidewalk to Carmody's left, watching. It had to be a fair fight.

"You're all bluff, Carmody," Howie said.

The gunman merely smiled. He reached up with his right hand to adjust his hat, appearing disarmed. It was then Howie made his move.

Carmody was faster, his right hand so swift that Howie didn't even see his draw. Carmody fired first, Howie second. The shots rang out loud, echoing.

Carmody, grazed on the left shoulder, barely reacted.

Howie dropped to his knees, firing again at the mud. Wild-eyed and dismayed, he grabbed his middle and shuddered, then fell facedown and rolled on his side.

People came out of doorways. Cox went to Howie, kneeling and turning him over onto his back. Howie stared up at him, squinting. The doctor came to squat down with Cox, but merely shook his head. Howie was gut shot, bleeding both inside and out.

Clay waved the crowd back and came to kneel with Cox. Both men suspected Carmody was too good a shot to have missed the heart.

"Howie, you're not gonna make it," Cox said quietly.

Howie just lay grasping his belly and staring up at the doctor.

"Howie," Cox prodded gently. "You got anything to tell us afore you die?"

"I deal from the bottom," Howie gasped, eyes wide.

"You shoot Jacob Turner?" Cox asked.

Unable to speak, Howie couldn't take his eyes from the doctor.

Cox tried to question him further, but no sound was forthcoming. There was a hush in the crowd standing on the far boardwalk.

Doc Miller was stone-faced, unable to save Howie, who finally died resting against Cox's big hand.

Miller silently got to his feet. He walked away, retracing his steps up the stairway to his office.

Carmody walked over to look down at Howie. He was grim but satisfied, still holding his left shoulder with his right hand, blood seeping through his fingers.

"He's dead," Cox told him. "You'd better get up to see the doc."

The gunman holstered his weapon and nodded. He wasn't smiling, but his thin black mustache curved up with the twist of his mouth. He turned and headed over to the stairs alongside the mercantile.

People gathered on the sidewalks. Men, women, and children wanted to see what had happened.

Cox looked over his shoulder at Carmody climbing the stairs. "You're not through with him," he said to Clay.

"I got no reason to fight him."

"He'll find one. Killing a Darringer would make him a mighty big man."

Cox signaled men to carry Howie to the undertaker's.

Clay walked back to the boardwalk and up toward the hotel. Jacob and Katherine were standing on the steps. She had her arms wrapped about herself, as if made cold by the sight of death. The crowd had gone its own way, and they were alone.

"What's Cox gonna do?" Jacob asked.

"Nothing. It was a fair fight."

They looked at the window above the mercantile, wondering if their imagination was out of bounds.

"Could be Doc had nothing to do with it," Jacob said. "Maybe Carmody just went after Howie to show what a big man he is."

"But he gut shot him," Clay pointed out. "That's the way the doc's son got it."

They were silent a long moment, knowing they would never have the answer. They turned and entered the hotel, wandering into the lobby area and finding seats alone against the windows. Katherine and her brother sat on a couch while Clay found a chair. Clay didn't like the distant look in her eyes.

"Doc lost his only son in a fight with Howie," Jacob said, "but he also lost his wife when they first come here a few years back. She died when some wild cowhands came charging into town and didn't see her crossing the street."

"Renshaw hands?" Clay asked.

"Sure was," Jacob said.

"Don't talk about it anymore," Katherine cried anxiously.

The two men looked at her. She was near hysteria. Jacob put his arm around her, drawing her to her feet. He took her upstairs. Clay followed.

In the hallway, they paused as Katherine went into her room, closing the door. Jacob turned to Clay.

"You having supper with us?"

"I'm going to sleep in the jail tonight," Clay said, shaking his head.

"And tomorrow?"

"I'll be at the trial. You think she'll be all right?"

"She's a Turner. She's tougher than she looks, and she knows what's right."

"Maybe, but it's not even two weeks since she was attacked and saw three men murdered. She was out of her mind from heat and shock. I don't know what'll happen on the stand if it all comes back to her."

"She's a Turner," Jacob repeated.

Clay shrugged and turned away. It was going to be a long night. He left the hotel and joined Cox.

Around midnight, with Simon the blacksmith's help, they brought a sleepy Thatcher over to the jail, shoving him into the cell next to Sheb.

"You ain't dead!" Sheb shouted angrily.

"No thanks to you," Thatcher grunted, hunching up on the cot. Once he convinced himself Sheb couldn't get to him, he promptly fell asleep.

Sheb was snarling while Thatcher was snoring. The blacksmith was allowed to go home for the night. Clay and Cox had just barely sat down to talk when there was a banging at the door. Cox, drawing his six-gun, went to the window. Then he opened the door to allow Tate Wiley to enter, keeping Tuck outside.

Tate was red-faced, his square jaw jutting forward.

"What's goin' on here?" he demanded. "I just found out you got my boy."

"Your son will stand trial tomorrow," Cox said, holstering his six-gun and returning to sit at his desk.

Clay remained seated, keeping an eye on the elder Wiley.

"On what charge?" Tate demanded.

"Murder of Sid Turner and his men, and attemptin' to kill Miss Turner," Cox said.

"That's a lie," Tate insisted.

"Miss Turner survived the attack. She recognized your son."

It took a long while for Tate to swallow the lawman's words. He looked at his son, then back to Cox once more. He slowly calmed down, his voice even.

"You only got one witness, and the jury ain't gonna believe her. I'll see to that."

"Pa, get me outa here," Sheb pleaded, grabbing the bars.

"Just relax, son," Tate said. "You'll be a a free man. They've got no real evidence against you."

"You goin' to cause me any trouble tonight?" Cox asked.

"I believe in justice," Tate said. "I'll see to it my son gets off free and clear."

"Pa, you can't trust the jury," Sheb argued, frantic.

"Son, when I was in the Army, I handled many a court-martial. I always won my case, so don't you worry. You're not going to be convicted on the testimony of a hysterical woman."

"But what about Thatcher?" Sheb asked.

"What about him?" Tate responded, surprised.

"He's liable to say anything," Sheb told him.

Tate walked over and looked Sheb straight in the eye.

"Son, are you innocent?"

"Sure, Pa, you know that. I told you, I just went to the line shack to do some thinkin' and maybe some huntin', that's all."

"Then you have nothing to worry about," Tate said, turning and walking toward the door.

"Pa, get me outa here tonight," Sheb pleaded.

But his father was gone, the door barred behind him. Sheb's face was ashen, his searing eyes round and wild. Desperate, he sat down on his cot, his face in his hands. At length, he lay back and fell asleep, snoring softly, drowned out by Thatcher's whistling breath.

"Well," Cox said, "I don't think anything's going to happen tonight. Tate thinks he knows so much about the law, he's probably looking forward to the trial. If he loses, then we'd better watch out."

"When's the judge get here?"

"Stage comes in about noon. We'll set up court in the hotel's lobby. Perkins coming?"

Clay nodded. They spent an hour discussing strategy. Then they took turns sleeping on the bunk.

In the morning, more food was brought in. Sheb Wiley glared at them, alert and restless. The blacksmith took up his post outside, seated on the bench with a shotgun.

Wiley was starting to talk, bragging that nothing was going to happen to him just because of some woman's vindictive plan. Thatcher was quiet, sleeping most of the time.

Before noon, Renshaw and his daughter came in by wagon. Cox went out to tell them about Howie. From the window, Clay saw the old rancher hunch up. Susanna covered her face with her hands. The wagon moved on down the street, Susanna hugging her father.

Soon, Tate Wiley and his other son rode into town, dismounting to enter the hotel. They walked tall and confident.

Before noon, the stage pulled up in front of the hotel. The only passenger was a man in a long black coat. He went into the hotel. There was a lot of activity as excited townspeople helped bring chairs into the hotel lobby.

"People like entertainment," Cox grunted.

"Well, they won't see much," Sheb called from his cell, "except you bein' made a fool of."

Soon, a merchant came to tell them that the court was ready.

The prisoners, handcuffed behind their backs, were moved into the street. People gathered to stare at the tough Wiley being herded through the mud.

"They're still afraid of me," Sheb snickered.

Half the town had already crowded into the courtroom set up in the lobby. Chairs were lined up and occupied. Two tables were set in front of the desk the judge would use. Off to the right side of the room, facing the bench, a dozen chairs were waiting for a jury.

Tate, his son Sheb, and Thatcher sat at the table on the left of the courtroom, facing the bench. Clay and the sheriff sat at another table on the right. The doctor and Tuck Wiley found seats. Perkins and Wes followed. The Renshaws found room in the back row as sympathetic townspeople moved.

Cox went back to talk with the judge, then brought him forward.

Judge Peabody was a short, stocky, mean-faced, no-nonsense judge who insisted on a quick jury pick. None of the jurors worked for Wiley. They were mostly townsmen.

A witness chair was set between the bench and the jury.

Thatcher's trial came first. Tate volunteered to be his lawyer. Cox was the prosecutor.

Perkins testified about the card games. "I kept beatin' him. Thatcher wouldn't give up. He could beat everyone but me. He figured I was cheatin'."

"Were you?" Cox asked.

"No, but he thought so, I reckon."

Clay testified about the gunfire from the alley, the footprints leading to the back door, and the mud on Thatcher's boots. Tate fought it as all circumstantial, pointing out that Thatcher had no rifle.

Thatcher insisted on getting on the stand. He claimed he had been mad at Perkins, but not that mad.

"Why were you in town that night?" Cox asked.

Tate objected to the question as irrelevant, and was overruled.

"I came to play cards."

"Did you play with Perkins that night?"

"No, he wouldn't play cards with me. Said he was tired of me. Everyone laughed when he said it."

"This was the night he was shot?" Cox asked.

"Sure was, I reckon."

"What did you say to Perkins?"

"Well, I told him if he didn't play cards with me," Thatcher said, "I was gonna beat the grin out of 'im."

"And what did he say to that?"

"He just laughed and said, 'Kiss my foot.' "

"And it made you mad?"

"Sure did."

"Enough to shoot him in the boot?"

"I didn't do nothin'," Thatcher growled.

"Did the Wileys ask you to shoot him?" Cox asked.

Tate violently objected and was overruled, but the prisoner insisted he had been fired for laziness and no one had paid him to do anything.

At Tate's urging, Thatcher did say he was an excellent shot and added that if he had wanted to shoot Perkins, he sure would not have missed.

The jury decided Thatcher had been mad enough to shoot Perkins in the leg and foot. They figured he had done it. However, thanks to Tate's arguments, they believed the man when he said his intention had not been to kill. They convicted him for assault and battery, declining to find it attempted murder.

"This court withholds sentencing until both trials are completed," the judge declared.

"Your honor, I object," Tate said. "This ain't right."

"Objection noted," the grim man at the bench replied. "However, this court has the power to delay sentencing at its discretion. Proceed with the Wiley trial."

There was a recess. The same jury was seated. Sheb was restless in his chair. Tate was confident, proud of having helped Thatcher. In fact, Tate was strutting a little as he and Cox stood up.

"What are the charges?" the judge asked.

"Murder, Your Honor," Cox said. "Sheb Wiley was responsible for killing Sid Turner and his two men, and for attempting to kill Miss Turner."

"What evidence are you presenting?"

"Testimony," Cox answered.

"Your Honor," Tate said, "I object to this trial being held in Castle Creek. I ask it be removed to Tucson so the accused can have a fair trial."

"Denied," the judge said.

"I also object," Tate continued, "on the grounds that there is no body. There's no proof Sid Turner is dead."

"Your honor," Cox said, "it's my understandin' an Army officer arranged the burial in Bravo Canyon. If you want to hold the record open, we could get that man to give us a declaration of some kind."

"Objection overruled. If the officer's testimony becomes necessary, this court will rule at that time."

"Then, Your Honor," Tate said, "I object to the accused bein' prosecuted by the arresting officer."

"Sheriff?" the judge questioned.

"No problem, Your Honor," Cox said. "Mr. Darringer can handle the questioning."

"Darringer?" the judge repeated, frowning.

"Clay Darringer," Cox explained. "He knows the case."

Clay was stunned by the sudden responsibility. Yet he knew that if Tate's request were denied, the martinet could claim it was not a fair trial.

First, Clay brought Thatcher back to the stand. The nervous man was cautious in his responses, giving very little information except that he knew there had been some night riding from the Wiley ranch.

Then Tate had his turn at Thatcher. The former officer stood tall and important behind the table as he spoke.

"Isn't it a fact that you were angry at the Wileys for firing you?"

"Well, sure, who wouldn't be?" Thatcher grunted.

"And isn't everything you just said about night riding a blatant attempt to get back at the Wileys?"

"No," the big man grunted. "They was bein' fair about it, givin' me a week to draw my pay and move on. But I didn't like it there nohow. They was always wantin' you to work."

Everyone laughed, and the judge pounded his gavel.

Clay stood up for redirect. He folded his arms, studying Thatcher, who was becoming nervous. So far, the big man had not been cooperative. Clay tried again, but Thatcher was still uneasy.

"Mr. Thatcher," Clay said, "if you have nothing more to say, the judge may as well sentence you to Yuma."

"Your Honor," Tate cried, "I protest. The prosecutor is badgering the witness. He's trying to get him to lie so he won't have to go to prison."

"Your Honor," Clay explained, "I'm trying to get Mr. Thatcher to tell the truth, but apparently, he can't figure out what scares him the most, the Snake Den or Tate Wiley."

The crowd laughed, and the judge pounded his gavel.

"Mr. Thatcher," the judge said, "I assure you that you have nothing to fear from Mr. Wiley. I know him to be a man of honor. And whether you expect a light sentence in return for your cooperation should not affect your telling the truth. You are under oath."

Clay stood between Thatcher and the Wileys, blocking the big man's view. Wiley protested, but was ignored.

Thatcher took time to think it over. He knew all about Yuma from friends who had been there. Sweat covered his brow and ran down his big nose. Finally, he clutched his hands together and nodded.

"Now then," Clay said, "did you see Sheb Wiley when he came back from Texas?"

"Yeah, last Friday, around midnight. He was out at the corral talkin' with some feller from Shanty Wells. Luke Boslow, I think. I'd gone out for a smoke, 'counta I can't stand bein' closed up in the bunkhouse at night, and they didn't know I was there."

"And what did you hear?" Clay asked.

"Sheb was tellin' him to go ahead and burn out the Turners."

"Hearsay!" Tate cried. "Inadmissible."

"Overruled," the judge said.

Clay asked Thatcher to continue.

"Well," he said, "then ole Sheb, he starts braggin' how he already took care of Sid."

"Your Honor!" Tate protested. "That's hearsay."

"Overruled," the judge ruled. "I'm allowing it as an admission, whether or not defendant was merely fabricating. The jury is instructed that what the witness heard may not have been true. The witness may continue."

"Well, I got to worryin' about what I was hearin'," Thatcher told them, "so I went back inside."

"Then what happened?" Clay asked.

"Well, nothing much," Thatcher said, "but the next evenin' when we fellas was gettin' ready to head for town for our Saturday night, ole Riggs was talkin' to Sheb on the porch, and pretty soon, ole Sheb comes and saddles up and heads for the hills."

"Then what happened?" Clay persisted.

"Well, then, old Riggs comes over and tells us we ain't to tell anyone Sheb was back. Afterwards, one of the boys what had been with Riggs said they had just seen Miss Turner and them gunfighters ridin' toward town."

"What happened then?" Clay asked.

"Well, them Texas boys that had come back with Sheb, they lost all their guts and saddled up, headin' for Mexico."

"And?" Clay prompted.

"Well, that's all I know."

"Do you know where this Boslow is now?"

"No," Thatcher said, "but he and some other boys from Shanty Wells been hangin' out at one of the line shacks. And there's somethin' else. When them fellas tried to kill me at the jail, one of 'em sure enough looked like Boslow."

Tate, white-faced, grilled Thatcher on re-cross.

"Are you trying to make this jury believe that you just happened to be out there in the dark and heard Sheb Wiley talking with this Boslow?"

"That's right," Thatcher said.

"When did you tell Sheriff Cox about what you heard and saw?"

"Well, the other night, it was," Thatcher told him. "He said if I cooperated, I wouldn't have to go to

Yuma. So I tole 'im what I knew and where I thought old Sheb might be, and he went and got 'im."

"You made up a story and had Sheb arrested?"

"It was the truth," Thatcher grunted.

"Your Honor," Tate said, "this is all perjury by this man in a clumsy attempt to get a light sentence."

"Your Honor," Clay countered, "I have faith in the jury's ability to consider all the testimony."

Tate Wiley continued to grill Thatcher, tearing at him every way he could, but the big man refused to change his story.

Frustrated, angry, Tate Wiley let the prisoner go.

Katherine was asked to take the stand. Jacob brought her down the stairs and to the chair between the judge's bench and the jury.

She looked as if she were under severe stress, clutching her hands together in her lap. Still wearing Susanna's dress, she seemed small and helpless, afraid to look at the sneering Sheb Wiley.

Clay asked her to tell what happened in the canyon in her own words. She didn't look at him. Silent, perhaps retreating to the trauma of the attack, she refused to speak.

Uneasy, Clay stood in front of her. Then he knelt, taking both of her hands in his, allowing her to keep twisting them within his grasp.

"Katherine," he said softly. "You must speak."

Slowly, she looked up at him, tears in her eyes.

"All right, Clay," she whispered.

Still, she looked only at the judge and Clay, refusing to look at Sheb. She related how she and her brother had been attacked before dawn and left to die with the two cowhands.

"A man put his hands on me. I tore off his mask. He kept at me. I shot him."

"Who was it, Katherine?"

Clay was still holding her cold hands. She hesitated. Her face white, she stared at him, then spoke softly.

"Sheb Wiley."

"Do you see him in the courtroom?"

Her eyes filled with tears as Clay smiled gently and released her right hand. She bit her lip, fighting for control. Clay squeezed her other hand. She drew a deep breath and suddenly pointed at Sheb.

"That's him," she said.

"After you shot him, what happened?"

"He clubbed me with his rifle. He thought I was dead."

"Were you ever aware these men were following you?" Clay asked.

"When Sid met me at Camp Grant, we saw the herd," she replied. "Sid went over and talked with the men. When he came back, he said one of the men was Sheb Wiley. We turned northwest while they were going directly north. Sid wanted to get away from them and took us to Bravo Canyon."

Clay grudgingly allowed Tate to cross-examine.

"Miss Turner," the stiff, military-style man began, pacing in front of her to add to the show. "Isn't it true that your brother had told you he suspected the Wileys were causing trouble for your family?"

"Yes."

"Isn't it true you had it in your mind that the Wileys were bad people?"

"Yes."

"Isn't it true that it was still dark when you were attacked?"

"Yes."

"Had you ever seen Sheb Wiley before this alleged incident?"

"Yes."

"How long ago?"

"Two years," she said.

"For how long?"

"Just to meet him. An hour."

"And with one hour's visit, you could remember his face after two years?"

"Yes."

"In the terror of the attack, isn't it true you didn't really see the man's face?"

"I saw his face," she insisted.

"Were you hysterical?"

"I think so."

"And so in the darkness, being hysterical and believing Sheb Wiley had been seen at Camp Grant, didn't you just imagine it was Sheb Wiley?"

"No."

Tate cleared his throat and continued. "Isn't it true you're making this all up?"

"No," she said, stiffening, suddenly brave. "Sheb Wiley was there. He was with the men that killed my brother. I saw his face. I shot him."

"Miss Turner, where did you hit him with the bullet?"

"In the chest, I think."

It was then that Tate became dramatic and had the doctor come forward to examine Sheb. Miller removed the prisoner's shirt, pulling it back down on his arms. There were no scars from bullet wounds on Sheb's hairy chest.

Sheb proudly displayed his strong body. Flexing his muscles, he turned to face the spectators, showing his unmarked chest. The judge ordered him to sit. Miller returned to his seat, and Sheb's shirt was pulled back on.

"Miss Turner," Tate said. "You didn't really shoot him, did you?"

"I pulled the trigger," she said, shaken.

"You didn't shoot anyone, did you?"

"I thought I did."

"You were hysterical, delirious perhaps. It's possible you didn't see any faces at all, isn't that correct?"

"I saw Sheb Wiley," she insisted, ashen and trembling.

"Miss Turner," Tate said. "You don't really know that Sheb Wiley killed anyone, isn't that right?"

"He was there," she said.

Tate smiled, hooking his fingers in his vest pockets. He strutted in front of her while Clay continued to kneel and hold her hand. Tate stopped suddenly, speaking coolly.

"We all know you loved your brother Sid. It would be understandable if you were trying to place blame."

"Save your comments for your closing remarks," the judge admonished.

"Miss Turner," Tate said, "do you like the Wileys?"

"No," she responded.

"Why not?" he persisted. "Are you afraid of us?"

"Yes," she said.

When Tate had finished trying to change her testimony and discredit her, the martinet was convinced he had won his son's case. He walked tall as he returned to his seat.

Clay asked her only one question. "When your brother was killed, who was the man attacking you?"

"Sheb Wiley," she said clearly.

Clay stood up, still holding her hand and pulling her to her feet. Shaken, still in tears, she fell into Clay's arms, hugging him with her face at his chest. Clay wanted to cry himself as he put his arms around her before passing her to Jacob.

Her brother took her back to her room, then returned to watch. Tate's closing arguments were centered on the fact that Sheb Wiley had never been shot. He claimed she had made up the story because she hated the Wileys.

Clay insisted Katherine had seen Sheb Wiley, even if her shot had missed.

"We submit," Clay said, "that Sheb Wiley came up from Texas with his herd and those 'Texas boys.' The five of them left the herd to follow the Turner wagon. They figured no one would ever know what they done out there, so they killed Sid Turner and his men."

Clay hesitated, feeling awkward. He looked to the

lawman for help. Cox merely nodded. Clay drew a deep breath and continued.

"Sheb Wiley thought he'd have his way with Katherine Turner. When she fought, he beat her down and left her for dead. We also submit that a man called Boslow was hired by Sheb Wiley to burn out the Turners and kill Mr. Thatcher."

Judge Peabody gave the jury instructions.

"Gentlemen, murder is the unlawful killing of one human being by another with malice aforethought. Malice aforethought is a man-endangering state of mind that is neither excused, justified, or substantially mitigated."

He further explained and gave instructions on conspiracy and hiring others to kill, but it wasn't necessary. The jury, having listened intently throughout, only had to whisper among themselves.

Their verdict was unanimous. The foreman, a bearded merchant, stood up, looking important.

"Your Honor, we find Sheb Wiley guilty of murderin' Sid Turner and his two men, tryin' to kill Miss Turner and ole Thatcher there, and of tryin' to burn out the Turners."

The judge leaned back, asking the prisoner to rise. Sheb was barely able to get to his feet. The prisoner was frantic, shaken, eyes wild, while his father was ashen and devastated.

"Sheb Wiley," the judge said, "before I sentence you, have you anything to say in your own behalf?"

"No, he doesn't," Tate answered for him.

Sheb straightened, trying to be as tall as his father.

He looked at the judge with searing eyes and nodded. "Yeah, I got plenty to say."

"No, son," Tate whispered.

"Let me caution you," the judge said, "that if you have no remorse, the sentence will be harsh. However, if you show grief for your acts, the court might be lenient."

"Sure I got grief," Sheb said. "I mean, we Wileys know cattle. We got the smarts to have the biggest spread in this territory. But the Turners, why, they wouldn't give an inch."

"Sheb," Tate pleaded.

"So it ain't my fault, Your Honor," Sheb said. "My old man wasn't doin' nothin', so I had to do it all myself. I had to do all the plannin' and ridin'. I even had to get those Shanty Wells boys to burn out them Turners. Then I set 'em on Thatcher 'counta I didn't know what he'd heard."

Tate was gripping the table. "Son!"

Sheb ignored him and continued. "I couldn't tell Pa 'counta he woulda stopped me. And I couldn't tell Tuck, 'counta he was too dumb to keep his mouth shut. And that's why I got stuck with the whole thing, Your Honor. I was the only one could handle it. I didn't have no choice. So it weren't really my fault."

Sheb seemed satisfied with his speech, his head held high.

"Are you finished?" the judge asked. When Sheb nodded, the judge leaned back in his chair, shaking his head. "That's not remorse, son."

"Your Honor," Tate pleaded, "he doesn't know what he's saying."

"I'm afraid he does," the judge concluded. "Sheb Wiley, I could sentence you to hang, but Miss Turner's testimony and that of Mr. Thatcher were not corroborated. Also, no corpus delicti was brought before this court. Justice will be served as well if you're in Yuma Prison for twenty-five years."

"Your Honor, we're going to appeal," Tate said, still shaken.

"The record is so noted."

"And I'll see the governor," Tate added, his voice fading.

"That's it, Pa," Sheb snarled. "You stick to your dumb books and writings and your blamed code of ethics, and you sit back while I rot in Yuma."

"Son, don't give up," his father said, red-faced.

"You and old Hack, livin' in the old days. Well, this is the way it really is, Pa. There's no field o' honor in this courtroom."

Tate was devastated, watching his angry son standing in fury at his side. They both sat down, a lifetime apart.

It was then that the judge had Thatcher stand.

"Mr. Thatcher, you are to abstain from gambling for one year. You are to work as a jailer for one year in the custody of Sheriff Cox. It's my understanding you will be paid a nominal sum."

Thatcher was confused. "But I'll be here where the Wileys can get me."

"No Wiley will come near you," the judge said. "Right, Mr. Wiley?"

Tate nodded, his face drawn and haggard.

Then the judge turned his attention to Cox.

"Sheriff Cox," Peabody said, "it appears you should do something about the men from Shanty Wells."

"We plan to do that, Your Honor," Cox affirmed.

The judge stood up, and everyone rose. Peabody left his bench and carried his notes to a back room.

Tate turned to glare at Clay. "You're the cause of everything that's happened here, Darringer."

"Let me get him, Pa," Tuck said from a row back.

The noise and clamor of people rising and stumbling over each other served to carry Tuck away from Clay and the lawman.

Jacob came to stand with Clay. Sheb Wiley was seated, his face drained of color, his eyes round and bright with anxiety. The sheriff, Clay, and Jacob escorted the prisoners through the crowd.

Once outside, Cox and Jacob took Sheb and Thatcher across the street while Clay stood guard in front of the milling crowd. The sun was shining brightly. The mud was thick in the street.

When the prisoners disappeared inside the jail with Cox and Jacob, Clay relaxed, but only for a moment.

"I'm gonna get you, Darringer," Tuck called from the hotel steps.

Clay turned with a grimace. "Listen to me, Tuck. I don't want anything to do with you."

"I'm not afraid of you," Tuck said. "I'll take you right now, if you're a mind."

Tate emerged from the crowd, putting his hand on

Tuck's shoulder. "Take it easy, son. First we gotta take care of your brother."

"And I'll take care of Darringer," a cool voice said.

Everyone turned to look at Carmody, standing just down the street, right out in the mud. The sun was bright on his silver conchos. Wearing black, he looked like death itself.

Clay knew men like Carmody. They weren't afraid to die. That's how they stayed alive, terrifying their victims with their own cool disdain for life.

Conscious of his sore right shoulder, Clay stood still a moment. He could think of better ways to die. A rocking chair came to mind.

"Back off," Clay said.

"I can't leave town till we settle this."

"Nothing to settle."

"You got a big name, Darringer. I aim to take it with me."

"I got no fight with you," Clay said.

Carmody smiled, his thin mustache moving sideways.

Deciding to ignore him, Clay started across the street toward the jail. The crowd was hushed, backing up the steps of the hotel.

Clay felt the call like a knife deep in his back.

"Darringer!"

Clay kept walking, his boots dragging in the mud.

"I'm gonna toss this gold piece. When it hits, you'd better draw, or you're dead."

Refusing to look at the man, Clay continued, but out of the corner of his eye, he saw the coin sailing in the air. He realized Carmody would still say it was a fair fight, whether Clay drew or not.

It wasn't the way Clay had wanted to die, flat in the mud in the face of some decorated gunman. He had begun to fancy a life on his own spread, sitting in that rocking chair with his grandchildren at his feet.

Clay paused and turned, watching the coin as it came sailing down toward the mud.

In that one split second, he saw Carmody's hand move.

As the coin hit the mud, the gunman drew. Clay's hand had already slammed his holster and brought up his six-gun, firing as he fanned the hammer with his left hand.

Carmody jumped in the air as the bullet hit his chest. His shot whistled past Clay's ear. The gunman gasped, his left hand clutching his middle. His black eyes were round and wild.

Clay lowered his six-gun, watching the gunman drop to his knees. Carmody was staring at him in disbelief. For a long moment, the gunman leaned forward. Then he fell facedown in the mud.

There was a long, breathless silence. Then men came forward to check on the dead gunman. Cox and Jacob had come out of the jail.

"Now it's my turn," Tuck called.

Clay slowly holstered his gun, watching the men who had knelt over Carmody suddenly rushing back to the sidewalk.

"Son, get back here," Tate said, frantic.

But Tuck wouldn't listen. He had always fancied

himself a fast gun. His boyish face was stern, dark searing eyes narrowed. He could avenge his brother and still be a big man.

Tuck walked tall as he moved onto the muddy street.

Chapter Nine

"**G**o ahead, Darringer," Tuck said, spreading his feet apart as he stood in the muddy street. The crowd on the boardwalk and hotel steps was hushed. The stage was set. Tate Wiley was ashen, trembling with anxiety.

"Go back to your Pa," Clay told him.

"Sheb was right, you know," Tuck said. "It's the sons gotta get things done. The old men are just too old."

Clay started walking toward the jail.

"Darringer, you see this?" Tuck shouted.

Tuck had picked up the gold coin from the mud. He bounced it in his hand, sneering, pleased at the uneasy silence of the crowd.

Clay hesitated, his sore shoulder bothering him. Yet there was something sinister and unsaid in Tuck's leering gaze. Maybe Tuck would fill in a few answers if taunted.

"You haven't got the guts," Clay said, turning.

"Just try me."

"If you'd have had guts, you wouldn't have let Jacob run you off when you wanted his sister."

175

"He didn't run me off!"

"What do you call it?"

"I figured she was too snooty, that's all."

"He didn't say you had no more brains than a tom-cat?"

Tuck's eyes were narrowed slits of fury. He wet his lips, glaring at Clay as his fist tightened on the gold coin.

"Well, I showed him, didn't I? And I'm gonna show you."

"You weren't dumb enough to shoot him down, were you?"

"I coulda killed him dead if I'd of been a mind to."

Tate took a few staggering steps forward. "Tuck!"

"Stay outa this, Pa. You always thought I was dumb, didn't you? Well, I was helpin' you get rid of Jacob Turner, that's all. You set so much store by ole Thad, you just never had time to see how smart I was."

"Son, stop your fool talk. They'll arrest you."

"Fool, am I? No one's gonna call me a fool after I kill Clay Darringer. Even better, he just done in Carmody. So you see, Pa? I'll be the man what got Carmody and Darringer. No one will dare walk in front of me, Pa. Not ever again."

"Son, let it be."

Tuck ignored his father and opened his sweaty fist to let the coin shine. Then he tossed it in the air. It caught the sunlight and started down in a spin.

Clay hesitated, his sore shoulder worrying him.

As the coin struck the mud, Tuck drew, but his gun never cleared his holster. Clay drew and shot him hard in the chest. Tuck spun backwards and fell on his side, rolling and gasping as he tried to pull his weapon.

Tate stumbled through the mud to drop at his side, pulling his dying son into his arms. The soldier couldn't cry. He just buried his face in his son's hair.

Clay was sick to his stomach. He looked at the crowd. Susanna was staring at him, her hands to her face. Hack Renshaw was putting his arm around her.

On the porch, Katherine was leaning on a post and looking lost from the world, her color drained.

The doctor came forward, but he couldn't save Tuck.

Tate Wiley lifted his lifeless son into his arms and staggered down the street with him. The rancher was humbled, shaken down like a mighty oak that had been chopped to the ground. One son was going to prison. Another was dead.

For a long moment, Clay's glance was fixed with Doc Miller's as the man straightened. They understood each other in that dark, thoughtful reflection. Without a word, the doctor was saying he had sent for Carmody. Yet he had not made the world perfect. And guilt had already set in. Clay wanted to reach out and put his hand on the medic's arm, wanted to tell him he understood, but all he could do was nod.

The doctor turned away, stoop-shouldered and weary.

Clay holstered his gun and walked over to Sheriff Cox, who opened the office door for him. Clay entered, his body covered with sweat.

He sat down in front of the desk, next to Jacob.

"I've got to get out of this town," Clay muttered.

"I must say," Cox said, "that you've done your duty."

"More than any man," Jacob agreed. "And if I can't get you to stay, at least you could have supper with us tonight."

Clay shrugged, looking at Cox and the prisoners. Sheb was seated in a cell, his face in his hands. Thatcher, his ankles chained together, was sweeping the floor and looking mighty content.

"When do you take Sheb to Yuma?" Clay asked.

"I got six men lined up to move 'em out afore morning. They'll be meetin' up with the Federal Marshal."

"What about Tate Wiley?" Clay asked.

"I don't figure he's got much left in him," Cox replied. "He can't help bein' an honorable man. But I think we'll be ready for him if he tries anything."

Clay turned to Jacob. "You'll be all right now."

"I sure hope so," Jacob said. "At least now I have a new brother to kind of help things go along. Katherine wants Wes legally adopted into the family. But what about you, Clay? Will you be joinin' us for supper?"

"No, I'll be spending the night here," Clay decided.

They discussed the trial for a short time. Cox told them the stage would be leaving at noon the next day, and the judge would be on it. Jacob left Clay in the jail with Cox and the prisoners.

It had been a long day. Clay was mighty weary and

sick of it all. Sheb was silent and brooding. Thatcher kept eyeing a deck of cards Cox was using to play solitaire. Clay merely shook his head and grinned.

"You know," Cox said to Clay, "you'd make a mighty fine lawman. You got integrity and honor."

"Thanks, but I figure on headin' west. And I think I might take up medicine again, when I have a chance."

"Thought you gave up the idea."

"I've been watching the doctor."

"He's a dedicated man."

"More than that. He's human. And I guess a man can be one fine doctor and still not be perfect." Clay settled back with his profound thoughts.

They spent the night taking turns at watch.

At dawn, Clay stepped outside to watch Sheb Wiley leaving with his six-man escort. The prisoner's father stood on the hotel steps, watching them ride away. Sheb looked back anxiously.

Clay suddenly knew that Tate was not going to do anything illegal to prevent Sheb's taking his medicine. Clay was gaining new admiration for this man.

The stage was soon in front of the hotel for loading of luggage, mail, and goods to be shipped. The judge would be leaving with it.

The town looked peaceful. Cold and silent.

As Clay crossed the street, he told himself he just wanted to see if Katherine had recovered. She had suffered plenty in the canyon and had relived it at the trial.

He walked around the stage and up the steps, entering the hotel lobby. In front of the desk stood Hack

Renshaw and his daughter. The luggage was obviously hers.

Susanna came forward to talk to Clay alone.

"I'm sorry about everything," she said softly.

"Why are you leaving?"

"This is no town for me. It's too violent. And so are you, Clay Darringer. I can't live with that. I'll never forget how you shot those men in the street."

"But your father's alone now," Clay pointed out.

"This is his idea. He'll be all right."

"No, he won't," Jacob said from behind her. "Nor will I."

She turned, staring up at him, unable to respond.

"Now that you got your mind off Darringer," Jacob told her, "maybe you'll stick around and pay attention to your neighbor."

Susanna was confused. "I don't understand."

"If you stay, maybe you will."

It took a minute for his words to sink in. Susanna's stiff pose slowly softened. She kept staring at Jacob. He could not take his gaze from her. Finally, she seemed to recover her feminine charm.

She smiled at Jacob, nodding. "Maybe you're right."

Clay, surprised but content and strangely satisfied, watched them return to her father. The three seemed suddenly close together. Her luggage was now on its way back upstairs. Maybe Renshaw was going to get Turner land after all.

But where was Katherine?

Worried, Clay started for the stairs, but was

stopped by Jacob. "Clay, what are you plannin' to do?"

"Just see if she's all right. Then be on my way."

"You're turnin' your back on somethin' mighty fine."

"Man gets involved, he can get hurt, Jacob. I've had my turn at that. Besides, your sister is loco."

Jacob just grinned as Clay hurried up the stairs and into the hallway, stopping at her door to pound on it.

The door opened. There she stood in a new dress the color of her eyes. She was smiling. Her red hair was drawn back from her lovely face. He was surprised to see her high spirits.

"I just wanted to see if you were all right," he told her.

"And why shouldn't I be?"

"Then I'll be on my way," he said, tipping his hat and backing off down the hallway.

She followed, still smiling. "You get back here, Clay Darringer."

"Not a chance," he said, backing to the stairs.

He lost his footing, stepped into space, and crashed down like a barrel, rolling all the way to the bottom step and landing in a heap. Katherine came hurrying down after him.

Jacob and the others came to his side.

Clay sat up, shaking his head. He hurt all over and had no breath. He looked up at Katherine's fearful concern.

Disgusted, he got to his feet and started for the

door. He was getting out of town and now. He'd get outfitted at Boxer's and head west.

He didn't look back as he charged into the street and headed for the livery. His heart was pounding as he reached the big open doors and rushed inside. His right shoulder still hurt, but he didn't need a woman to rub it down.

As fast as he could, he saddled his roan. Before he could mount, he heard a woman's voice. Knowing it was Katherine, he stiffened, cold sweat all over him.

"Clay Darringer, you're not leaving until you explain something to me."

Slowly, he turned, exasperated. "And what's that?"

"Just tell me. What's wrong with me?"

He stood looking at her beautiful face with its freckles, at her shining red hair, her grass-green eyes, and her splendid form.

"Nothing," he admitted.

"Then why are you running away?"

Clay hesitated, looking her over, remembering her kiss in the hallway of her home. He recalled the way he had cared for her when she was ill. He thought back to the way she had shot the Apache. She had a man's courage. She was beautiful. She was part owner of the prettiest land he had ever seen. Why was he running away?

"I'll be darned if I know," he said.

She smiled, moving closer. "Do you want me to be sweet and demure and afraid to speak?"

"No."

"Do you want me to keep my thoughts to myself?"

"No."

"Do you want me to let you do the courting?"

"No."

"Then what do you want, Clay Darringer?"

Clay drew a deep breath, gradually admitting what he really wanted, aside from medical school. He wanted love, a ranch with a wife and children. The answer was here, holding out her arms. All he had to do was gather his strength and courage and take that terrible leap into her glistening web.

Removing his hat, he shook his head. He knew he'd never have a handle on this woman. She would drive him crazy. But he sure would love every minute of it.

He grabbed her and pulled her into his arms, crushing her up against him. She threw her arms around his neck. He kissed her hard and fast. She kissed him back.

And his fate was sealed.

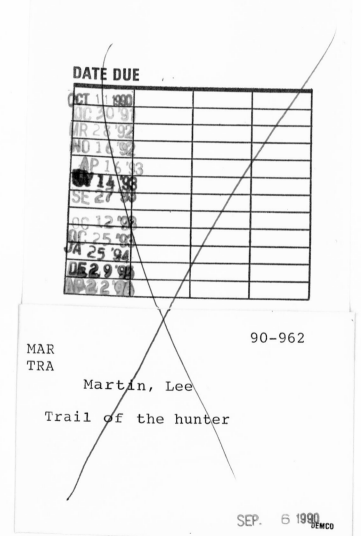

E.

Rm